BIG RIG

Ω

Published by
PEACHTREE PUBLISHING COMPANY INC.
1700 Chattahoochee Avenue
Atlanta, Georgia 30318-2112
PeachtreeBooks.com

Cover design by Maria Fazio
Interior design and typeset by Adela Pons
Edited by Jonah Heller

Printed and bound in June 2022 at Thomson Reuters, Eagan, MN, USA.
10 9 8 7 6 5 4 3 2 1
First Edition
ISBN: 978-1-68263-252-9

Cataloging-in-Publication Data is available from the Library of Congress.

LOUISE HAWES

BIG RIG

PEACHTREE

ATLANTA

FOR THE SUPER SIX, WITH LOVE:
LILY, REGAN, CAYLA, STEPHEN, ANDI, AND OWEN

—L. H.

My father drives an eighteen-wheeler. My mother died a week after I was born. And even though this is *not* a ghost story, the three of us have been on the road together for seven years.

I don't mean that Mom is some shapeless blob of ectoplasm or that she rides in her own seat, moves furniture around, and talks to us from the ether. I mean that, ever since I was little, Daddy and I have traveled with a green marble box with her ashes inside. I mean that my dad loves her so much, and I dream and think about her so often, it feels like she's part of our team.

So yes, all three of us have logged over 560,000 miles, spent the night in 310 cities, and listened to 1,430 audiobooks. I know because I handle the GPS, read the maps (Daddy says technology is fine, as long as you don't count on it), keep the logs, and, since my father is all for equal votes on entertainment, choose half the books we listen to.

Which is why I also know I might have to change that audiobook total back to 1,429. (I like to keep really accurate log data, but I hate to erase things that leave smudge marks for weigh-station fussbudgets to cluck their tongues over.) Why am I seeing smudge marks in my future? Because just now, headed east on 80 toward Iowa City, my father pulled onto the shoulder of the highway and yanked a CD out of the deck after only a few minutes. It was my turn to choose, and I was really looking forward to *Zombie Lullaby,* which I think is a great title. In the opening scene, there have already been three bloodcurdling murders, one excellently scary undead villain, and a severed head that doesn't talk but just rolls around moaning and looking beseechingly at everyone it bumps into.

Maybe the head was too much for Daddy, because now he leans across the cab and waves the disc in front of me. "You're eleven years old, Hazel, for-crying-out-loud," he says. "And this book is much too violent."

I decide not to mention that my birthday is less than six months away, which makes me almost twelve.

When my father, who's tall and mostly arms and legs, makes big, I-know-what's-best-for-you gestures and gets in my face like this, our truck's cab feels way too small. Normally? It may not be wide enough for jumping jacks, but there's plenty of room to read, sleep, and eat. Suddenly, though, I need more space; I want to look out the window, find tiny doll people riding in the four-wheelers down there, or watch the sky and highway streaming past like they're caught in a windy river.

Instead, I sit up straight, look Daddy right in his eyes, where I can reach him. "How about we at least get to know the main characters?" I ask.

My father used to be an English lit professor, and he's always talking about how the people in books are what make the difference. "People, not plot." He says that all the time.

Now he just shakes his head, half smiles. "Good guys or bad?" he asks.

I look at the green marble box Velcroed to our dash. "Let's ask Mom," I say.

We're both quiet. We look toward the box, swirly and elegant stone on the outside, ashes sealed inside. And we wait.

"She says either one will work," I tell Daddy after a while. He sighs, then hands me the CD. I put it in, and we turn back onto the highway and listen to *Zombie Lullaby* for another twenty minutes. There are more murders. More rolling heads. And more undead villains, who all say the same thing: "You must die!" Over and over. And over.

We're about three hours from the world's largest truck stop off Iowa 80. (I love the pulled pork sandwiches there, and Daddy likes the vintage trucks at the Trucking Museum.) Which means we have more than enough time to hear the rest of the book. But, sad to say, those villains have gotten pretty boring. And it turns out, Mom was right. It doesn't make any difference which side I choose—the good guys are just as boring as the bad ones. First of all, they keep dying off. And second, they repeat things, just like the zombies do. There's a detective who can't be very smart, because she keeps telling her friends, "I'm close. I know I'm close." And of course, she's right. She *is* close . . . to her own grisly end. But I don't have the staying power to see how and when she meets the same fate as the rest of the townspeople.

I press PAUSE and look at Daddy. "Okay if I turn this off?" I ask him. "I can't invest in this." (That's professor talk. It means *There's no one to root for.*)

My father's smile grows from half to full-on. He can't turn to face me because the traffic's too heavy, but it's plain to see, even in profile, how relieved he is. Once again we've settled one of our problems by letting Mom decide things. We do that a lot.

Sometimes I think I remember my mother. In dreams, she holds me with one hand and runs a finger down my newborn nose with the other. I hear the sound of her voice, as if it's happening right now, not eleven years ago: "Don't grow up, Hazel Denise Sampson. Don't you dare grow an inch! I want you just like this forever!"

But Daddy and I talk about her so much and paw over those old photos in the glove compartment so often, I can't be sure which are real memories and which are things I've heard or made up. What I know for sure about Mom is that she couldn't have been much like me: for one thing, she had thick red hair, not mouse brown. (Daddy insists my hair is "skinny blonde," but that's just plain wishful thinking.) In the picture I like best, Mom's wearing a white blouse embroidered with roses, and her hair? It's even brighter than all those flowers put together.

Another thing I'm sure about is that she was smarter than Daddy, and he's the smartest person ever. Not just because he's got a PhD, but because he's taught me everything I know (except the lyrics to One Dimension songs). He can recite the whole last act of just about any Shakespeare play. And he can prove that everything in the universe is growing, including dirt. If *he* says my mother could think and talk circles around him? I believe it.

Her name was Glory, which sounds more elegant than Hazel. And *way* more elegant than Hazmat. That's my trucker handle; drivers almost never use their real names on the road. Ever since Daddy's boss and best friend gave me my nickname, hardly anyone calls me Hazel—unless they're mad at me. "Hazmat" is short for "hazardous materials," so you can probably guess that, in the beginning, at least, Mazen Shields of Shields Trucking didn't think it was a very good idea for Daddy to take me on the road. In fact, he figured it was downright dangerous.

I was only four the day Daddy asked Mazen about driving with me. That was the first time I ever heard the two of them disagree. "Anything could happen, Blake," his friend told Daddy. And trust me, he didn't mean anything *good*. All the big trucking companies feel the same way; they have strict rules about family and ride alongs. But Daddy and Mazen have been friends forever, and Daddy didn't see why a two-truck firm couldn't bend the rules to let his cute but too-small-to-see-out-the-window-without-a-pillow-in-her-car-seat daughter go with him.

Apparently, though, there were lots of reasons. "Hell," Mazen told Daddy, "if they don't get you for truancy and endangering a minor, Hazmat here could end up with colic, or crawl under a wheel, or get lost at a truck stop, or—"

"Four-year-olds don't get colic, Maze." According to Daddy, Mazen worries way too much. According to Mazen, worrying is in his blood.

Even though they're like brothers and went to high school and college together, Daddy is white and Mazen is Black. Which means only one of them grew up with what Mazen calls Daily Advisory Warnings. "My mom wouldn't let me out the door," he says, "'til I recited the three rules: 'watch your front, watch your back, and never, ever talk back.'"

The day they fought about me, Daddy took a deep breath and slowed down, like he's always telling me to do. But his voice still got way too loud, and he used his fingers to count all the ways Mazen was wrong: "You can't be a truant if you're not old enough to go to school." (Pointer finger.) "You've taken Shepherd on the road, and my daughter is a lot smarter than a puppy, for God's sake." (Middle finger.) "And if Hazel gets lost, I'll get lost with her." (Ring finger.)

My father stopped at three fingers, then took them all down to put his arm around me in a bear hug. "We're a team, right?"

I turned into a pre-K bobblehead—grinning and nodding, grinning and nodding.

I was so busy nodding and smiling, I hardly noticed when Daddy took his arm off me and put it around Mazen. When he pulled him close and told him not to be such a worrywart, that he'd already promised my mom he was going to be both a father and mother.

But Mazen folded his arms and shook his head. "And me?" he asked. "Where does what *I* think figure in all this?"

Daddy started to answer, but Maze held his hand out in front of him like a tight end with a football. "First of all, Hazmat's the closest thing I've ever had to a kid of my own. And if *you're* not going to worry about her, somebody has to. Second, in case you've forgotten, it's my company. And third, it's my truck. It's not you that's going to pay the price if some busybody at a weigh-in station wants to know why she's not in kindergarten!"

There were lots more arguments. And sometimes both Daddy and Maze forgot to follow my father's rule about taking a deep breath. In the end, though, Mazen agreed to bid some really short hauls to give his new "team" a chance to prove ourselves. And Daddy agreed that we'd always stay at Mazen's house in between runs.

The day we drove off on our first job, I didn't even know enough to realize how much I was going to miss Mazen and his wife, Serena. I just clutched the bear Serena gave me for the trip and waved at them from my perch in the passenger seat. I'd already taken short rides in Daddy's high-as-a-house truck, and I couldn't imagine anything better than living in it for good.

Seven years later, I still feel the same way. Sure, Leonardo (that's what we named our rig) doesn't seem quite as gigandous now as when I was four. And he's what you'd have to call a senior citizen truck. At over twenty years old, he's missing some bells and whistles, as Daddy calls them. But who really needs a built-in microwave or heated seats? Besides, age has its advantages—trucks as old as Leonardo don't need to use Electronic Logging Devices, which means my paper logs are just fine; not to mention, our truck tends to get lots of compliments. Other truckers stand around and admire the paint job Mazen spent a fortune on and the chrome exhaust stacks. "Great rig," they tell Daddy. Or "A long nose Pete—now there's a classic!"

So I wouldn't trade being homeschooled by my dad in a traveling classroom, or falling asleep in my top bunk under the glow-in-the-dark constellations he's put on the roof of the cab, or meeting old friends at every truck stop, or swinging between coasts like a pendulum—I wouldn't trade all that for anything. Anywhere. Ever.

Which brings me to growing up. I've decided to postpone it indefinitely. Daddy says that when I'm older, we'll quit trucking and buy a house just like Mazen's. He gets all poetic about the barbecue grill in our future backyard, about the four-poster bed in my future bedroom, about all the warm, accepting fellow classmates in the future public school where I'll finally blossom into my "full potential" because of "group learning."

When he goes on these imaginary journeys into tomorrow, my father's voice changes. It gets loud and sounds like the computer voice that asks you to hold and listen to music while you wait to talk to an actual person. I can tell he's not really that excited about public education or quitting trucking. Or splitting up our father-daughter team. But he's so convinced that I need other kids and teachers in my life—and he works so hard at describing how I'll love every future minute of it—that I haven't found a way to tell him I'm not going anywhere without him.

Instead, I play along. "So, when I'm in junior high," I ask, "can I dye my hair blue?"

"Ask your mother," he says.

I look at the box on the dash. "Mom?" I listen for a minute. "She says sure."

Daddy shakes his head, smiles. "It figures." He says it kind of sadly, kind of proudly. "That's just like her."

THEY DON'T MAKE THEM LIKE THEY USED TO

I'm going to name my rig Gaddy. That's short for gadabout, which is a neat word my friend Yoli taught me. Daddy and I met her in a really bad restaurant in Denver about a year ago. We all three agreed that the "Deluxe" Lasagne wasn't. Then she told us she used to drive with her husband, but now she's on the road by herself. "I sign on for easy jobs, take my time, go where I want, when I want. I'm a real gadabout."

Of course, Daddy knows every big word that's ever been said or written, so he just nodded. But I needed to know. "*Gadabout?*"

"Sure. That's someone who doesn't have a strict timetable. No place they have to be. They just keep moving."

That's when I knew what I'd call my truck. Because Gaddy and me? We'll be just like that—fancy and free, mile after mile.

Gaddy will be an eighteen-wheeler just like Leonardo. And before you go all "girls-can't-drive-trucks" on me, you should know that Daddy and I have met plenty of other women drivers. It's just Yoli's the only one I email.

Whenever I have good Wi-Fi and no homework, I check in with Yoly <yolandasmendez@flashserve.com>. She signs all her emails "Yoly the Road Runner," and she thinks Gaddy is a great name for my truck.

I'm glad I have Yoly to write to. She's funny and smart and tough. Plus, I need all the support I can get, considering my own father doesn't even believe in Gaddy. "It's not that I don't think you could drive if you want to," he's always telling me. "It's just I'm not sure you'll get the chance."

I've heard this before. "You mean robo-trucks, right?"

Daddy nods and tightens his grip on the wheel (if we're on the road) or on my hand (if we're not). "I think we need to make plans, that's all. We need to adjust."

What my father means by "adjust" is get into that house with the barbecue and the girly bedroom. He's afraid that by the time I grow up, no one will need truckers at all. He thinks we're replaceable. And he's not the only one. When we first took Leonardo on the road, not too many truckers worried about computers doing their jobs. But now, every other stop, someone's talking about it. And the talk is never good.

Take tonight. We get into Iowa City just in time for dinner. The shiny plastic menu is about ten feet long, but of course I already know what I want. I've been looking forward to a pulled pork sandwich for miles, and the one I find in front of me is dreamily delicious. I carry that tangy, sweet taste with me to the truck museum, and it lasts until the man in charge walks over to chat with Daddy about the 1914 Pierce Arrow dump truck they're both clearly in love with.

"You don't need a program to drive that one." The man is tall and stringy and speaks slowly, like words are jewels and he doesn't want to let them out of his mouth. Which means he doesn't look or sound one little bit like a driver. (Most of the truckers Daddy and I meet are pretty hefty from loading freight and eating on the road, and every one of them loves to talk.) Still, Mr. Forsythe (*Patrick Forsythe, Museum Director,* his badge says) must like the way my father has walked all around the antique dumper, how he's crouched down to read the information beside it. "Perhaps we'll have to put a driver on exhibit one day," he tells us.

My father stands up, nods at the hand crank on the old-fashioned truck. "Couldn't run *that* without man power," he agrees. "Wonder how long we'll be able to say the same thing about the rigs out there." He points to the parking lot outside, to the hundreds of trucks—tractor trailers like ours, flatbeds, reefers, tankers—all lined up, row after row after row.

The museum manager folds his arms, considers the ranks of trucks beyond the window. "What are you driving?" he asks.

"'99 Peterbilt," Daddy tells him. "We did a rebuild eight years ago."

"Ahhh!" Mr. Forsythe smiles as if Daddy has just mentioned a secret password, and they bump fists. "Great air rides. And those long noses make service easy, huh?"

"That hood's light as a cloud," my father says, grinning back. But now he points an accusing finger at the model of a new automated rig with a modern, streamlined cab, a snub-nose grill, and *no driver behind it.* "The wave of the future here, on the other hand, requires a password and a can opener just to get inside."

Mr. Forsythe is nodding and sighing, and my pulled-pork happiness is fading fast. Does "wave of the future" mean it's all true? Can computerized trucks really put Daddy and me and all the drivers we've met out of a job?

"Come on, Daddy." I remind my father I'm here by tugging on his flannel-covered elbow. "It's showtime."

My father tears himself away from the exhibit, and we head to the gift store to get a movie we can watch in the theater upstairs. Not many truck stops have their own theater, after all, and neither of us is even a little bit curious about the rest of *Zombie Lullaby,* so we ask the woman at the register for a trucker movie. She hands us *Smokey and the Bandit,* which is an amazing film, but honestly? My father and I must have watched it forty kazillion times.

"Do you have anything a little . . . newer?" I ask.

The woman, who's already staring past me to the three people in line behind us, checks the list she keeps in a book under the register. "*Smokey and the Bandit Two?*" she says.

Daddy and I look at each other. We've seen that one, too.

The woman smiles, not very patiently, then shuts the notebook. "How about *Smokey and the Bandit Part Three?*"

That's the sequel that the star of the first two movies didn't even show up for. Daddy and I have seen it, too, of course. But once was definitely enough.

"Hey, mister." One of the people in line is a lot more patient and a lot more friendly than the cashier. "I feel your pain." He's a heavyset man with his hair pulled back in a ponytail. He's with a lady who must be his wife (wedding rings, matching Mayflower Moving shirts), and they're both holding big boxes with train sets on the covers. "But you're gonna have to settle for the oldies but goodies if you want a decent trucker film."

"Guess so," Daddy says. "The seventies and eighties were the high point."

"Do you mean the 1970s?" I'm back to elbow tugging. "You were just a little kid then, right?"

The man's wife nods. "I remember the first time we saw *Convoy*. Those big rigs riding to the rescue! That handsome Kris Kristofferson!" She smiles up into the other man's face. "Why, that movie changed my life. It's the reason I decided to join my hubby on the road."

"Can we watch that one?" I ask Daddy. I love the song "Convoy," and even though Daddy's sick of hearing it, I'm thinking the movie, along with plush seats, popcorn, and Sour Patch Kids, might be a great way to get ready for bed.

"Sorry, Haz." Daddy points to the cashier's book. "We'll have to settle for the classic." He pays for *Smokey I* and explains to the couple behind us, "I just told my navigator here that we couldn't listen to a zombie story because it was too violent."

"It was just a few murders and a severed head," I explain.

The other driver takes my father's side, of course: grown-up tag team. "Yep," he says. "*Smokey*'s fun, but *Convoy* can be pretty scary..." He pauses, thinks it over, like he's watching that old movie in his head. "Not to mention the language."

That decides it. Daddy stopped using our CB radio as soon as I got old enough to ask about all the swears. He put the CB in a duffel bag. Now? We can't find that bag anywhere. When Daddy wanted to check out fuel prices in Spokane last year, we took the truck apart, but the duffel was gone—along with my magnetic dollhouse, Christmas reindeer horns for Leonardo, and the CB.

Daddy's always telling me, "Pick your battles." As near as I can figure, he means that asking for one thing you can get is smarter than asking for lots of things you can't. "Okay," I say now. "I kind of like watching that mean sheriff get all worked up anyway."

So even though we know the sheriff will lose and the Bandit will win, we check out the film, and as we head upstairs, the man and woman with the train sets wave.

When we get to the tiny theater, Daddy and I find we have the place all to ourselves, so we get to play Goldilocks: we pick out seats that are not too close to the screen and not too far, but just right. Then the fun starts. We set up the popcorn between us, and we get ready to say the best lines right along with the actors on the screen. Burt Reynolds plays a big rig driver, and of course he has a handle, the Bandit. His best trucker buddy is Cledus, whose handle is Snowman, and who drives with his dog, Fred. In the beginning of the movie, Snowman gets on his CB to talk about the crazy load they'll be hauling. Daddy speaks Snowman's part right along with the actor. "Me and Fred have a question," he says. "How come we doing this?"

I take Bandit's part. "Well, why not?" I ask.

Now Daddy and Snowman get to the point: "Well, they said it couldn't be done."

Me and Bandit: "Well, that's the reason, son!"

Daddy and Snowman: "That's good with Fred. We're clear."

Daddy and I laugh, then do the CB sign-off together with the two actors on the screen: "10–4!" we yell, slapping hands.

It's like that through the whole film. When you've watched something as often as Daddy and I have seen *Smokey*, all the good lines stick in your head, like the lyrics to a song you know by heart. So we keep right on jumping in and speaking for Bandit and even for the evil but very funny sheriff, who wears a mustache and looks like a cartoon villain. It's like listening to a story that scared you when you were a little kid, but now you know everything will turn out fine. You don't mind seeing the drivers and their friends get into scrapes and fights, because they're going to have the last word and come out on top—rounding tight corners, smashing through police barriers, and flying over broken bridges, all from the sky-high cab of their shiny, powerful rigs. (All the trucks in those days were "cabovers," so drivers sat on top of the engine compartment. And if that wasn't actually sky-high, it certainly made them kings of the road!)

I'm saving my yellow Sour Patch Kids for later, but our popcorn's all gone by the time Bandit and the Snowman have done what they came to do. As the credits scroll across the screen, Daddy and I sing our hearts out to "East Bound and Down."

We've got tears in our eyes from laughing so much and cheering so hard. When the lights come on, we're feeling like we can take on the world. Daddy turns to me, jabs a thumb at the empty screen. "They don't make them like that anymore," he says.

And me? I take out my first yellow Sour Patch Kid, let it melt in my mouth, and wonder, *Why not? Why doesn't somebody make a movie like that?*

MONSTER TRUCK

It's a good feeling to wake up excited to get on the road. There's only one more haul until we head to North Carolina to see Mazen and his wife, Serena. I grew up in their house, so it feels like coming home every time we go back. The only trouble is, that doomsday talk we heard yesterday? It starts up again first thing this morning.

Daddy is just climbing into the cab when the driver of a mega-rig parked next to us stops him. He taps my father's shoulder and hands him a map that's fallen out of the door pocket. "Doing things the old-fashioned way, huh?"

The man has long red hair and an ancient baseball cap he's wearing backward. He points to the map, grinning, all teeth. Because it's just a joke, my father smiles back. "My network drops me so many times," Daddy explains, "I bet I check this thing three times a day."

"You mean *I* do, right?" I take the map from him and put it with the others in my pocket on the passenger door.

"I stand corrected." Daddy's words always get longer and fancier when he's teasing. "Allow me to introduce my daughter and Chief Navigator, Hazmat."

"Cool handle, Hazmat." The other driver salutes me through the window on my father's side of the cab. "I'm Fast Lane." He takes his cell phone out of his jacket and waves it at the pile of maps beside me. "Hey," he says. "Guess it won't make much difference how we get from here to there. We're all gonna be out of a job soon, anyway."

My father nods. "Welcome to the age of obsolescence."

The trucker stops, probably confused by Daddy's spelling-bee vocabulary. But then he plows ahead. "They already got a whole robo-trailer fleet down to El Paso, hauling appliances south on I-10." He tugs on his ear, as if he wants to shake something out of it. "Drivers like us are polar bears, man. We got nowhere to go."

Me? I can't stop staring at Fast Lane's truck. His tractor is not only higher and wider than ours, it's covered with so much chrome that light is bouncing off it in starbursts. There's a hood ornament on the front, a gold elephant breaking out of a silver egg.

"Truckers are a dying breed." The man's still talking, and now I'm actually listening to what he says. "Oh, they'll pay a few drivers to push brakes and clutch buttons in their high-tech control centers. But the rest of us?" He pockets his cell phone and sighs. "I give us five years—maybe ten."

No! It's all happening much too soon. I want to tell Fast Lane he's wrong. Dead wrong, he *has* to be. Gaddy isn't childish make-believe or some dumb imaginary friend. But I need the chance to make her real. In a few years I'll be old enough to drive myself, and I can be a real partner to Daddy. But now this driver with the neatest hood ornament I've ever seen is telling me I won't have time.

Since most grown-ups are sure they know more than I do, I don't say anything to Fast Lane. I just wait for my father to switch on his college-professor smarts and blow this guy out of the water.

Instead, Daddy shakes his head. "It's happening at warp speed, isn't it?" he asks. "Robo-trucks, self-driving cars." He sighs, too, and leans out his window toward the other man. "You think we'll be off the road and on the dole before our kids are grown?" He winks at me over his shoulder when he says the word "kids."

I know what that means. It means *I love you*, but it also means *This is an adult conversation*. So I stay out of it. I listen politely while the two of them carry on about the end of life as we know it. And when they've finished with doomsday talk, the other driver asks the same questions everyone does: How long have the two of us been on the road? Where's my mother? When am I going back to school?

Daddy and I get these questions all the time. There are lots of husbands and wives who team drive, and plenty of truckers ride with their dogs. (We've seen cats in cabs, too, and we met one driver who rides with his pet cockatoo.) But father-daughter pairs? In the seven years we've been hauling, I've never seen another one.

Daddy gives the same answers he always does: he doesn't mention Mom dying a week after I was born, and he sure doesn't show Fast Lane the green marble box on our dashboard. But he says that he and I have been a trucking team since I could sing "Itsy Bitsy Spider." He explains that he homeschools me. He says I keep better logs than he does. (I guess he means those extra columns I add to keep track of audiobooks, the restaurants we like, and how much exercise we get at rest stops.) He says I'm a big help. (More winking.) He says he wouldn't know what to do without me.

I should feel proud. I love it when Daddy talks about our teamwork. But I can't stop thinking about control towers and starving polar bears, and most of all, robo-trucks. Pretty soon I'm picturing the enemy up close and personal. The dazzling grill on Fast Lane's rig fades away. In its place, I imagine a monster: a giant tractor trailer, long and black with no company name or logo in sight. You can't stand on its running board because it hasn't got one. You can't climb into the cab because there are no doors. No windows, either, so you could never ride up there, watching the country wave back at you like a flapping crazy quilt.

This is not a monster truck from road rallies or TV. It's much bigger—bigger than Leonardo and the flashy truck parked beside us. It's not shiny or clean, it's dripping oil like blood; and it's *mean*. It makes faces at me the whole time Daddy and the other driver are talking. It can do this because even though it's missing doors and windows and mud flaps with bathing suit models on them, it *does* have a *face*! It looks like a mask made of shiny, ink-colored Legos. There are great clinking eyes that stare just over my head and a mouth that doesn't quite move in time with what its tinny computer voice says. And what it says is "STAND BACK; I AM DRIVER-FREE . . . STAND BACK; I AM DRIVER-FREE . . . STAND BACK . . ."

"Hazmat?" Daddy is looking at me as though he's been talking to himself and only just now realized it. "You okay?"

I look up to see that the other driver is already pulling out and my father has finished programming our GPS on the cell. He hands the phone to me and then puts Leonardo in gear. But I don't want to ride with a monster in my head, a monster that means the end of Daddy's and my life on the road.

"Can I ask you something?" I wish we weren't underway. I wish Daddy could turn and look at me. Really look at me.

"It isn't about ratios," I promise. (He must have explained the math behind those word problems fifty bazillion times, and I'm still not getting it.) "Or about putting 'Convoy' on our playlist." (I've been bugging him for three days to play that old trucking song, which would mean he'd have to listen to me singing along for miles.)

"Okay, shoot," my father tells me. But he's already checked the mirrors and is backing out of our spot. He lets a pickup filled with dogs and kids pass us, and then we're on the entrance ramp. I don't think he even knows it, but my father squints and makes a tiny o-mouth every time he hits the splitter button and breaks into fifth gear. So I don't ask him right away. I check the map against the GPS and wait until we're back on the highway and he's made that lemon-tasting face that gets us up to full speed.

"It's about driverless trucks." This is important, so I slow down, take a deep breath. "I know you say people won't always need truckers, right?"

Daddy nods again.

"But I didn't know that could happen in *five years*!" I remember the redheaded driver tugging on his ear, shaking his head. "I won't even be old enough to take the CDL by then!"

As often as I've practiced with sample tests for the Commercial Driver's License, I'm pretty sure I could ace the written part right now. But I may never get to prove it if robo-trucks put drivers out of a job so soon. You're not allowed to take the test for real until you're eighteen. Maybe I'll have to grow up after all. And fast!

"It might not be quite that soon," Daddy tells me. He keeps his eyes on the road, puts his teacher voice on. "Cultural institutions take a while to break down."

"Dad!" I'm not like Red in the baseball cap. "What are you *talking* about?"

"A way of life," he tells me now. "Trucking's a whole way of life."

"I know." I think about Yoly the Road Runner. About all the other drivers we've met on both coasts and in between. About racing snowstorms, driving into sunsets, and actually finding the ends of rainbows.

"But it's a way of life that's dying." Daddy's voice sounds as sad as I feel.

"Or is it just changing?"

"Maybe," he says. "Maybe. But we still need to make plans, Hazel. We need to adjust."

He means a house, of course. And settling down. I don't see how he can sit there, hands on the wheel, and even *think* about quitting trucking. Maybe it's all those classes he used to teach, classes where stories always followed a neat structure, with a beginning, a middle, and what he calls a "resolution." That's where everything gets wrapped up and settled and *over*. Who needs *that*?

CARMEN

When my father starts talking about "adjusting," I know it's time for me to have a heart-to-heart with Mom. We're halfway to Lansing before I get the chance. A downpour starts, and Daddy pulls over once our wiper blades are doing more harm than good. He stares at the giant, dirt-colored smear across the window. "I meant to change those," he says. "Can you check for the nearest auto parts store?"

"Sure." I take the cell phone out of its cradle on the dash and press the GPS search button. "Next exit, two blocks on your right," I tell him. I double-check the satellite map. "And they've got a big lot, with plenty of parking." Which is how I end up talking to Mom while Daddy's strolling the aisles of Big Al's Auto. I watch through the rain while he picks up a giant wrench and turns it over, feeling its weight. (Daddy loves tools, and he's never met a wrench he didn't like.) When I'm sure he's under the spell of all things must-have and shiny, I turn to the green box of ashes on the dash, then open the glove compartment underneath. I fish one of the hospital pictures of Mom out of the pile. It's the one where she's reaching out to touch a very tiny baby in an incubator. The baby (guess who?) looks pretty miserable. But Mom? She is *so* happy—even though we're hardly touching, even though she's wearing plastic gloves and I'm only hanging on to her finger with one of my scrawny pink hands.

Pretty soon I'm telling the photo all about Gaddy. My father has heard me describe my dream truck lots of times, but he's stopped listening. He's too busy "adjusting" to care. Now that I have the chance to talk to someone about it, I can't stop. "If I was driving Gaddy now," I tell Mom, "we'd save Leonardo for short hauls. Your box would be tucked into a custom cushioned dash, and there would be a window for the top bunk. We'd have a shower, and a driver's seat that swivels, and closets tall enough to hang everything."

I look at the woman in the photo. I can't see her eyes because her hair is hiding them. But I can see her smile, and I can feel it, too. "I haven't decided about a hood ornament yet," I tell her. "There was a driver in Des Moines who had a coiled cobra. And today I saw an elephant hatching out of an egg."

I double-check the auto parts store, then look back at the marble box. "So, what do you think?" I tell Mom about the pink bedroom my father wants to squeeze me into. About the smiling peers waiting for me in high school. "Why would Daddy want to retire us before I've even had a chance to drive?"

I want to make her see how much the road means to me, but Daddy is back too soon. He's got a new pair of wiper blades and a set of socket wrenches. While he's changing the wipers, I put Mom's picture away and stow the new wrenches in the tool drawer under my seat. The rain is coming down hard now, and we're going to need those wipers. I watch Daddy work from behind big, heavy drops that hit the window hard and turn into hundreds of tiny rivers cascading down the glass at crazy angles. "I mean, who wants to keep waking up in the same place every day?" I whisper to the box, soft and low so he can't hear. "And what do we need a backyard for, anyway?"

When Daddy has thrown out the old blades and climbed into the truck, he shakes his head like a wet dog and sends water shooting everywhere. I grab a towel from in back, and when he's dried off, he turns on auxiliary power. "Let's see what they're saying about this storm." He spins the radio dial, looking for a weather station, but stops before he finds it. He doesn't seem to care about the rain anymore. He just sits there, his hand still on the dial, listening to a woman sing in another language. "Oh, Lord!" Daddy says. "That's the Habanera."

"The Haba—what?" I listen to the song, too. It's fast, furious, and the woman's voice is throaty and laughing at the same time. "Is this an opera?"

"Yep." Daddy is smiling now, humming along. "And it's one of your mother's favorite songs. She used to sing it all the time." He chuckles, takes his hand off the radio, and runs it through his sopping hair. "Badly. Very badly. Glory never *could* carry a tune."

Mom's favorite song? Mom's favorite song! "What language is this?" I ask. "What is she singing?"

"The opera is called *Carmen*." For a man who just got soaked to the skin, my father looks incredibly happy. "It's written in French, but it's about a young, beautiful woman in a small village in Spain. Everyone's in love with her. The whole town wants her to get married and settle down, but she's telling them she won't. She never will."

I listen to the voice on the radio. "Why?" I ask. I have this prickly, waiting feeling, like you get before Christmas. "Why doesn't Carmen want to settle down?"

"Your mom used to say Carmen prefers stars to chandeliers." Daddy looks at the radio, then looks at me. "She wants to sleep under the sky, not a—"

"—fancy canopy?" I can't help jumping in. I know Daddy thinks I'd get used to a home that stays in one place, but my mother knows better. She knows I sleep under the stars and that I love it that way. I picture the long-tailed constellation my father has taped over my bunk. I'm not sure how she did it, but Mom definitely got my message!

"Love is a wild bird." That's what Daddy says the words to the song mean. "No one can tame it. Even when you think its wings are clipped, it flies away."

Carmen's voice bubbles like a fizzy drink. "What's she saying now?" I ask.

"My French is a little rusty." My father smiles, listening to the bubbles, too. "The bird you thought you caught by surprise," he says while Carmen sings, "it just beats its wings and flies away . . ."

A sweet, rainy patter fills the cab, and Daddy and I sit out the rest of the storm listening to a gadabout sing.

SCHEHERAZADE

We haven't been to Lansing in over three months, but the truck stop off 27 feels as familiar and friendly as ever. We're here to say hi to an old friend and to eat at one of our favorite restaurants. And not that you asked, but we're also here for the free showers!

Showers are much better on the road than they are in most fancy motels. For one thing, the big stops have a whole crew who do nothing all day long but scrub the stalls every time someone uses them. For another, you get your own key to your own private shower, with sparkling tiles, fresh towels and soap, and a mirror. And yes, it's all free, on account of Leonardo is a gas guzzler, and we get points for free stuff every time we stop for fuel.

Since we're visiting someone special, I take my newest jeans and tee into the shower stall with me. I hang them on the hooks over the bench and then get the water as hot as hot can be. I love standing under that see-through tent of steamy water. I love it so much that, of course, Daddy is finished with his shower and waiting outside for me long before I'm done. "I think you just set a record," he says as we head outside. "While you were in there, the weather changed!" He grins. "Nice shirt, though."

I love the shirt I'm wearing, partly because I've never seen another one like it, and mostly because every big rig navigator should wear one: I DON'T ASK FOR DIRECTIONS, it says, I *GIVE* THEM. And Daddy's right about the weather, too. It's as if the rainstorm we outran as we drove here has caught up with us. The restaurant we're headed for is only across the parking lot, but I don't want to lose the fresh, brand-new feeling I walked out of the shower with. I spot a newspaper someone's left on a counter under the plateglass window by the door. I hand half to Daddy, use the other half to hold over my head, and then we make a run for it.

Our destination? A rambling, pink stucco building with a giant letter *G* made out of winking bulbs and the word *Gyros* lighting up half the sky. But as we scramble in out of the rain, I wonder if Heifitz and his dog are still running our favorite restaurant. Each time we stop to say hello and to scarf down the best fried cheese on the planet, the old man insists he's going to retire. He tells us how he and Scheherazade will move to the suburbs any day now; how they'll buy a house and lie around in hammocks, eating halva and giant chew bones.

Daddy never got to see his own father retire. Both his parents were sick, sicker than he knew when he was a little kid. But they held on until he graduated college, and then they had to be moved to a nursing home. I never knew either one of them, but I picture Heifitz whenever I imagine my grandpa.

"Ya, ya!" Heifitz comes over to our table as soon as he sees us. Clearly he's still in business and still full of smiles, like always. He hands us each a clean dish towel to dry off with but pretty much ignores how we've already dripped all over his fancy purple plastic booth. "How is my favorite road team, huh?"

"Great, Heif." Daddy lights up when he sees the old man. "We're great."

Heifitz clamps one of my father's hands between his two beefy ones, then grabs mine next. "You see the world yet, kid?"

I laugh the way he wants me to. Which saves me from having to answer a question I don't really understand. Every time we visit, he asks me about the world, and every time, I know he means something bigger than more truck stops. Daddy and I have met a few drivers from Canada, and we talked to one who drove flatbeds in Mexico. I look down at Heifitz's feet, then under the counter by the newsstand. "Where's Scheherazade?" I ask.

Now Heifitz's whole face—his eyes, his mouth, his squirrel cheeks, everything—loses its shape and sort of collapses onto his shoulders. That's when I start to figure things out, and I wish I could take back my own question. Hammock or no hammock, something has changed since our last visit.

"Scheherazade." He says it as if he's forgotten his bloodhound's name, as if he has to learn it all over again. "She is dead." He closes his eyes, traveling to a place he doesn't want to go. "Since January."

For a minute, it's so quiet I can hear the grill hissing in the kitchen and the rain hitting the skylight over our heads. "My wife, rest her soul, she always hate the dog. Say hair everywhere, no good for business."

"I'm sorry, Heif." Daddy looks at me, not at our host. "I'm so sorry."

I can't help it. My eyes go right back to the newsstand by the checkout counter. That's where Heifitz's old dog would always greet customers. Gyros didn't need a hostess, not with Scheherazade on duty 24-7. "Take these nice people to table three," Heifitz would tell his bloodhound. Or, "There's a good view from number six."

And sure enough, you'd find yourself following a dog with a very large tail wagging at you all the way to your table.

"At least she never take sick." Heifitz shakes his head, gray locks still curly from the damp kitchen. "Only go slower and slower 'til one day, she just stay asleep."

"She was a great dog, Heif." Daddy glances back to the newsstand, too. As if he can't believe Scheherazade's not there.

"Ya." Heifitz is wringing his own dish towel so tightly, it looks like he might tear it apart. "Just go to show—enjoy what you got, while you got it." Now he and Daddy are both looking at me. "And *who* you got. You know?"

When Heifitz has gone back to the kitchen and the waitress brings our order, Daddy doesn't eat. "Hey, Hazmat," he says. He's staring at me now, as if he thinks we might get separated in a big crowd and he needs to remember exactly what I look like. He picks up a glass and holds it out in toasting position.

I clink my glass against his the way I always do, but Daddy doesn't make a toast. Instead, he puts his glass down again, and suddenly there are tiny tears at the corners of his eyes. "Hazel, I need to tell you something."

Hazel, not Hazmat. I have the clenched, wrench-tight feeling in my stomach that I always get when Daddy uses my real name to make one of his "announcements." (The last time was when he told me I'd missed so many questions on my pre-algebra final, we'd have to start the whole unit over.) Finally, just when I've decided to put my gyro out of its misery, he grins. "I like who I got," he says.

My stomach unclenches, and I pick up my fork. "I do, too, Daddy," I tell him. I think of Scheherazade, the way Heifitz used to tie her long ears up in a blue bandanna. And then I think of the green box in the truck and the soft crying sounds I sometimes hear at night when Daddy talks to Mom.

Maybe Scheherazade is showing off her bandanna to my mother right now. I picture Mom's long red hair from all those photos and a pair of big, sad bloodhound eyes looking up at her. I think about asking the green box if death is just a door, with my grandma and grandpa and all the people and animals who've ever lived crowded in behind it where we can't see them. When I get answers from Mom like I did today or when I dream her arms around me, I figure that's the way it works. But until I'm sure, this growing-up thing is still a problem. Sometimes I just want to stay a ratty-haired kid and sleep under plastic stars forever.

The hitchhiker is a girl. Older than me, but still not an adult. She stops us just as we're coming out of Heifitz's place with a giant takeout box. (Trust me, if you don't stock up on dolmades, you'll miss them for miles.) She follows us right up to the truck, then taps Daddy on the shoulder and gives him a sob story about her lonely father who's waiting and waiting for her to come home.

She's wearing this stadium-sized tee with a rotted-away picture of a band called Rageaholics. I can hardly believe it when Daddy tells her we'll take her as far as Grand Rapids. Maybe it's because it's still raining? Or maybe it's because every other word she says to him is "sir."

She doesn't even seem surprised; she acts like she *expected* us to give her a ride. She climbs up into the cab as if she's been doing it all her life, then plops herself on the bottom bunk behind our seats. "My name's Willa." She grins at me the way people smile at little kids they think they can sweet-talk into liking them. "What's yours?"

We've got a rule about hitchhikers, Daddy and me. *No. Never.* Okay, *almost never.* I mean, there are times when somebody stops us at the pump with an alibi that's just too complicated and sad not to be true. Like the man who was trying to get to his sister's funeral in January when his car broke down, and the garage told him it would take a week to get fixed, and he didn't get paid until next month, and he never finished telling us his story on account of he started crying so hard he couldn't talk.

If Daddy drove for a big trucking company instead of for his friend, we wouldn't even have to make a rule, the company would have one already. And it would be pretty much the same as ours, only stricter: *No. Never. Period.*

"I sure wish my dad drove a truck like this one," Willa says once we're underway. When I don't answer, she keeps right on talking. "'Stead of him lying in the hospital and all."

Daddy doesn't turn around, but you can tell by the way his right shoulder gets higher than his left and his eyes find her in the mirror that he wants to. "I thought you just told me your father is at home by himself, and that's why you need to get to Indiana."

Willa, who's thin and reedy like her name, looks at me like I should help her out. I don't. She shakes her head then and stares Daddy down in the mirror. "What I mean is, he *was* in the hospital. 'Til yesterday. Now that he's out, he needs constant care, you know? Twenty-four seven, on account of he's so weak."

Weak is what her lie is. And if I know it, Daddy *must*. Still, he just lets her win the staring contest and asks me to reroute the GPS and get out the maps. "It'll be a pretty easy haul from Grand Rapids, straight up 131," he tells the mirror. "Sorry we can't take you all the way. We're dropping off in Denver."

What he doesn't say is that we should be driving straight to Kalamazoo and saving more than forty miles.

"That's cool." Willa takes some breath mints from her backpack and holds the plastic case out to me. I shake my head, and she empties two of the orange mints into her own palm, then puts the case back. "What are you carrying?"

She sounds like she knows trucking, like she's done this a lot. What she doesn't sound like is someone whose father is dying.

"All right now," Daddy says. "We're picking up hardwood flooring in Grand Rapids."

Willa blinks. "Oh," she says, bored. "I once hitched with a guy whose trailer was filled with Ping-Pong balls." Now she's grinning, like she actually had anything to do with some driver hauling air. "They blew them into the truck, then sealed it up."

Daddy shakes his head, smiles. "Unloading must have been something."

"Yeah," Willa tells him.

Suddenly and much too fast, my father drops down about a zillion gears to avoid a Mustang that nearly cuts us off. "Sorry, ladies," he tells us, then makes a less than kind remark about four-wheelers that try to pass a whole truck in half the space they need.

"That's okay, sir," Willa tells him. "I've seen cars trying to make an exit ramp and turn across three lanes to do it."

Daddy shakes his head again. "I bet folks missed a lot fewer turns before cell phones." He's back up to speed now and turns on the radio. "Any requests?"

"Led Zeppelin?" Willa says it like she listens to '70s songs all the time. And of course Daddy eats it up.

"Now you're playing my tune!" He paws through our discs. "Forgot about some of these. Hope you don't mind going down memory lane. It could be a long trip."

"That's fine, sir." Willa's trying to sweet-talk my father, just like she did me. But in Daddy's case? It's working a lot better.

Our hitcher, out of trucking anecdotes, leans forward in her seat now and expects me to entertain her. "So, where's your mother?" she asks. She checks to make sure Daddy's still occupied with riffling through his musical past, then lowers her voice. "Are your parents like, divorced or something?"

I am *so* not going to explain about Mom's ashes in the box on our dash. And I am definitely not looking for sympathy from someone who's already put mud all over the carpeting by our bunks—someone who should get a logbook to keep track of her lies.

"No," I tell her, then throw her own hot potato right back at Miss Into Everybody's Business. "What about *your* mother? Why isn't she taking care of your father?"

Willa looks at me, confused, so I refresh her memory. "Your SICK father? Right?"

"Oh." She seems almost grateful for the prompt. "Well, my mom can't help out, on account of she's, you know, dead."

My stomach splits in two and crawls inside itself. "Dead?"

"Yeah. She got cancer when I was in first grade, and she died when I was in second."

Does this girl even know a lie from the truth? Does she even deserve to be talking about dead mothers with Mom's box not two yards from her long legs, her grimy sneakers, and her know-it-all attitude? I, for one, have no intention of feeling sorry for her. Not now. Not ever. Grand Rapids can't come soon enough.

When we stop an hour later, our passenger is sleeping so hard she's snoring. She's curled up like a baby around her backpack, her elbows all pointy. And dirty. Daddy looks at me, I look at him. Finally I reach out and touch Baby Willa on the shoulder. "We're here," I say. She takes her time surfacing, turns over, recurls. I touch her again. "Hello?"

This time she rubs her eyes and sits up. Maybe because she's still not fully awake, she forgets all about her seriously ill father. "Can't I go the rest of the way with you?" she asks.

"It's not raining here, and we're right off the highway," Daddy tells her. He's pulled into a rest stop and points to the three trucks parked in front of us. "I'll make sure you find a safe ride."

Willa scans the traffic that's making a dull ocean sound from the highway, then studies the trucks lined up by the overlook. "Listen."

Her voice sounds wobbly, uncertain. "I'd rather stay with you guys." Is she going to cry?

"We're going to Denver," I remind her.

She looks at me, shrugs. "I like Denver." She says it like we're at 21 Flavors, and she'll take pistachio if they're out of chocolate.

Daddy has finally caught on. He's got the door open, but he puts one leg on the running board and leans back into the cab. "So why did you tell us your father was sick?"

"That's why you gave me a ride." It's practically the first sentence out of Willa's mouth that hasn't ended with "sir," but she's right. I know it, and Daddy knows it. We both go quiet.

Willa sniffs. "You wouldn't like the truth nearly as much."

"Try me." Daddy's voice is soft like it is when I've missed a homework question, but he really, really wants me to get it right.

"My father's an effing psycho." Willa's not looking at either one of us now. She's fiddling with the straps on her pack, and I figure if she twists them any tighter, she's going to rip them right off. "If I go home, he'll kill me." Her head is bent, and you can't see her eyes. But her shoulders are shaking so hard, it's a safe bet she's crying.

Willa doesn't know what a good deal she's stumbled into. Daddy is always saying the only downside to my being homeschooled in a truck is that I never meet other kids. So it's a safe bet that even though Willa's just used a word he wouldn't let *me* near, Daddy's going to climb back in the truck and there'll be three of us on the road for a while more.

He does. . . . And there are.

SLEEPOVER

Willamette is her real name, but that fancy name doesn't fit with her wrinkled tee, which looks like she hasn't taken it off in weeks. It doesn't work with her hair, either. We spent the night at a truck stop on the other side of Grand Rapids, and when she woke up this morning, she didn't even run her hands through it. She just jammed it back into a silver clip that has dusty pink poodles all over it. Poodles!

She's still acting like she thinks she's my big sister, like even though I've spent every waking hour with my dad for the last seven years, she's going to slip right into our family picture—and *pushy total stranger makes three*. Really?

The drive around Lake Michigan is one big Willafest. She can't stop talking about herself, about how she's hitching to Hollywood to be an actress; about how she used to play the piano before her father sold it to buy a motorcycle; about how she's trained her dog to sing and to walk backward.

We eat dinner at one of my favorite places on the water, but our gabby tagalong manages to spoil everything. I make sure Daddy and I are sitting next to the dock, while Willa has to settle for watching the lake over the back of my head. "Sorry," I explain. "But my father and I have to feed the fish. It's a thing."

When she stands up, though, Daddy shares some of his dinner roll, and she tries to feed the whiskered channel cats that have popped their heads out of the water. She makes these loud sucking noises like she's kissing the universe, and at least half the fish disappear into the glassy reflection of the sunset.

"Now look what you've done," I tell her. "They're not used to you."

My father laughs and says he doesn't think catfish much care who feeds them. When a waitress comes to take our orders, though, Willa forgets all about the catfish. She looks at the menu as if she can't decide whether to eat it or read it. Then she chooses stuff like she's ordering her last meal—two appetizers, a main course, a side of fries *and* another one of onion rings. My father lets her order it all, then watches while she leaves half the food on her plate.

"Why did you order onion rings," I ask Miss Piggy, "if you aren't even going to finish them?"

Daddy raises one eyebrow at my soup bowl, and I grab a spoon and load it up with chowder, even though the croutons aren't floating on top the way they're supposed to. They've gone all soggy, and it tastes like I'm swallowing slime.

We usually save some of my assignments for the hour we drive after dinner. Which is fine with me. That's bound to be a Willa-free zone, right? I mean, how can Miss Onion-Rings-for-Brains possibly have anything to say about my homework? She isn't the one who's visited four mosques, two AME churches, and three synagogues for our unit on comparative religion. And she isn't the one who got 99 percent on the test Daddy gave me last week.

But the minute we're on the road and my father quizzes me about what happens in a Jewish service, Willa starts talking about this temple in this movie she's read about. She's in the back seat, of course, but that doesn't keep her from unbuckling her seat belt and waving one of her movie magazines in our faces. She carries a pile of fan zines in her backpack, and now she's found one with a picture of two actors outfitted like Aztecs standing in front of zillions of gold steps. At the top of the steps is an altar where, Willa confides in a stage whisper, the handsome pair in loincloths and peacock feathers are about to get sacrificed to the gods.

Daddy loves old-time films, I like fantasy (I'm looking at you, *Princess Bride*), and of course, we both love to watch trucker movies on the laptop we stow in back. But I don't recognize either of the stars in this picture, and I push the glossy photo away. "That's not the kind of *temple* we're talking about, Willa." I sigh like she's the most hopeless case ever, which she is. Daddy, who seems to have forgotten he ever taught English literature, doesn't even try to set our third wheel straight. So it's clearly up to me.

"I don't suppose," I ask Willa, "you even know the difference between polytheism and deism, do you?" I turn around in my seat, look at her sharply. "How old are you, anyway?"

"Fifteen," she says. She folds up the magazine carefully, then slips it back into her pack, as if she's stowing away jewels.

"Well," I tell her, "that makes you four years older than me." I sigh again and turn back to the road. "You should know better."

Willa is quiet until we stop for the night. That's when Daddy announces he's going to let "our guest" have his bunk and he'll sleep in the front with the seat collapsed. My father is six feet, three inches tall, and Leonardo has an extra-wide cab just so his toes will have wiggle room when he lies down. Willa, on the other hand, is not much over five feet. You'd think a thank-you would be in order, right?

Wrong. Because the world apparently owes her, Willa just yawns and asks for money to buy a toothbrush. "I hate that fuzzy feeling if I don't brush," she says.

"Then maybe you shouldn't run away," I tell her. "Life on the road isn't for everyone."

But Daddy just hands her three dollars, and then we all make our bathroom run. Willa stops off at the Zip Store on the way, and when she gets to the Ladies', I nearly laugh out loud. She's standing at the sink next to mine unwrapping a pink Tinker Bell toothbrush—a fifteen-year-old with a brush that's sprouted fairy wings! Then I remember her poodle barrette. I guess pink is her color.

When we get back to the truck, Willa puts her feet up and stretches out across the bottom bunk. And of course when Daddy says it's bedtime, she insists she's too excited to sleep. "Besides," she says, "I'm a little old to go to bed at nine." Then she asks all sorts of questions about where we're heading tomorrow and how the loading will work. Like she's so fascinated with the fine points of warehousing floor tiles, she'll burst if we don't discuss them right now.

Daddy starts telling her about load bars and lifts, things I've got firsthand experience with. But then he stops and points at me. "Time to put my brilliant but very sleepy daughter to bed," he says. He jackknifes and ducks into the back of the cab. "I saw you nodding off during my compelling discussion of pallets, Hazmat." He pulls down the bunk ladder. "Up you go."

My father and I have a bedtime ritual. It started when I was little and he put those glow-in-the-dark stars over my bunk. That's when he taught me about Ursa Major and Ursa Minor, constellations with fancy Latin names that mean "Big Bear" and "Little Bear." He said that long ago, before there was English or cars or cell phones, people made pictures out of stars in the sky. Then they used those pictures like Post-it notes to figure out where they were and how far they'd traveled, stuff like that.

Tonight, like every night, my father touches the tail of Ursa Minor on my sparkly ceiling. "Good night, Baby Bear," he tells me. I sort of wish he'd whispered it, not said it out loud. I mean, he might as well sing "Twinkle, Twinkle, Little Star." The Wide-Awake Teenager sitting right underneath us has probably decided I have the maturity of a kindergartener.

Daddy is standing halfway up the bunk ladder now, one hand on Ursa Minor, the other on my nose. He's smiling, waiting. Like every night for the last seven years.

Slowly I raise my hand. I touch the Big Dipper, but my voice comes out a lot quieter than I mean it to. "Good night, Papa Bear." I give him an air-kiss and I close my eyes so he won't say anything else. He stands there a minute, as if he has more to talk about. But finally he slides my curtain and clicks it shut, then backs down the ladder.

RUNAWAY

Closed eyes or not, there's no way I can sleep with those two talking so loud. Willa's still in the back seat, so I can hear all the brainless remarks she's making as clearly as if she were right here in this bunk with me. I can also hear my father, patient as ever, explaining that things don't work exactly the way Willa thinks they do. Then, when she tells him how strong she is, how she helped her neighbor's son move his drum kit, and how she'd love to drive one of those "little golf-cart thingies" at the warehouse that load and unload trucks, I've heard enough.

"No!" I sit up in bed, unfasten my curtain, and slide it wide open to make sure she can hear me. "You *cannot* use a forklift tomorrow." I can see Daddy's shocked expression in his rearview, but I keep going. "In fact, you can't get anywhere near the truck or the pallets if the warehouse guys are using forklifts."

I guess Willa thought I was in dreamland already, because she looks just as surprised as my father. "But I—"

"But nothing," I tell her. "Unless you want to cost somebody their job or even their life, the best way you can help with the loading is to stay as far away as possible."

And since I have their attention now, I inform the two of them that I'm not sleepy anymore and that I want to make sure Willa's newbie mistakes won't cost us time and money tomorrow. "So here's what needs to happen," I tell Miss Know-It-All. "You'll wait in the truckers' lounge while my father straps the load and I get the papers signed. Okay?"

That's when Daddy slaps the wheel. "Here's what *else* needs to happen, Hazel," he says. (Uh-oh. *Hazel.*) "I'm finished modeling common courtesy. And you're finished being rude." He gives me his best Voldemort glare, and I have to admit, it's a little scary. "If you don't want to go to sleep, we'll all listen to a book." He reaches into the box under the CD player. "Because it seems you're not able to hold a conversation without going straight for the jugular." He leafs through the CD cases, pulls one out. "How about *Jane Eyre?*"

Jane Eyre? I've only heard it a thousand gazillion times. And besides, we always save that one for my birthday. I am about to explain these things, patiently and calmly, when Willa decides, once again, to make a total jerk of herself.

"Ohhhhh. What a great cover!" she purrs. She studies the picture on the CD, then reads the description out loud. "A hapless outsider finds her true love, only to discover he hides a secret too dark to share."

She hands the case back to Daddy. "Yes! Let's play this one, sir. But I bet I already know what the secret is!"

I dangle my feet over the bunk, stare at her. "It's *Jane Eyre*, for crying out loud," I tell her. "We all know what the secret is!"

"Ohhhh! Don't tell me!" Willa has clearly never even heard of the book. And Daddy, who's watching her emote all over the place, is clearly going to play it for her. "Company chooses," he says, and drops it into the deck.

I give up. I zip my curtain back and lie down in the dark. "There was no possibility of taking a walk that day...." The familiar words of the story, the actor's soothing voice, they wash over me, and somehow, somewhere between Lowood School and Thornfield Hall, I fall asleep. When I wake up, Jane has already met Rochester and is hard at work tutoring her new pupil.

But something's wrong. The volume is turned down, and I hear voices speaking right over the recording. I open my curtain just wide enough to peek through and see that Willa has moved up to the front passenger seat, *my* seat. She and my father are talking. Or rather, Willa is talking—way too loudly and way too angrily.

"You can't call the cops!" She's nearly screaming now. "I told you stuff I've never told anyone." She points at Daddy, shoving her finger at his chest. "I trusted you, and now you're *ratting me out*?"

I'm about to inform The Guest Who Stayed Too Long that nobody but me talks to my father like that when Daddy himself shuts her down: "Hey." He puts one of his own fingers in front of his lips. "Shhhhh. I want to listen. But I don't want an eleven-year-old to listen along with me. Okay?"

Willa is doing that sob-choking sound you make when you don't want to cry.

"Listen to me." Daddy sounds serious. "There are some battles a kid shouldn't have to fight by herself." He lowers his voice, and I have to strain to hear him. "You've hitched through three states to get away from him, and I'm not about to let you go back alone."

Get away from who? How long have I been asleep?

More sobbing from Willa, and a new, even softer voice from Daddy: "If what you've told me about your father is true, you'll never have to see him again."

"*If* it's true?" Willa is yelling now, raw. "I didn't need to tell you any of this stuff. Are you calling me a *liar*?"

She may be angry and loud, but for once I'm pretty sure Willa's telling the truth. I know Daddy doesn't want me to hear this, but I can't help it. Quietly, quietly, I unsnap my curtains and slide them open a crack, just enough to see their shapes in the dark.

"No," Daddy says now. "I'm not calling you a liar." Then he lowers his voice and tells her something that, even with the curtain open, I can hardly hear at all. Something about "the authorities," something about making sure no one can hurt her.

This does not calm Willa down. "You can't!" She's equal parts scared and mad now, yelling again, twisting toward the door. "You can't tell the police. I won't let you!"

Running away to be a movie star is one thing. But running away to escape your own father? Willa's story just got a lot more complicated and a lot sadder than I thought it was.

She keeps yelling, blaming Daddy for making things worse. My father points up to my berth, hushes her as if she were a baby. But she's not listening anymore. She twists in her seat and opens the cab door. In one fluid, practiced move, she's outside and running across the parking lot.

Me? I'm down from my bunk before Daddy even turns around. When he does, we both move at the same time, climbing out of the truck and chasing after Willa. She's headed for a picnic table in the middle of the grass strip on the far side of the lot. Daddy and I split up around the rows of other trucks, and I get to her first. I grab Willa's arm and I don't let go. "Hey," I tell her. I'm breathing so hard I can hardly get the words out. "Don't you brake for friends?"

She's still shaking, but she lets me steer her to the table. I sit next to her, then Daddy catches up and collapses on the bench across from us. "We only want to help," he says.

It's too dark to see her clearly, but I can tell by the way her eyes shine that Willa's crying. "If you go to the cops, my dad will kill my dog." She gulps like a fish or a mermaid, something that doesn't know how to use air. "He says if I ever tell anyone about him, he'll poison Sasha."

"Sasha?"

Now she's crying for real—hoarse, broken sobs with little hiccups in between. I just sit beside her, wait for her to finish. When she finally stops, something has changed. It's like she's run out of places to go, people to lie to.

"She's part collie, part setter, mostly mutt." Willa sounds softer, less prickly. "No one else can get near her. I'm the only one she trusts."

Her voice is so low, I have to lean close. I can smell that filthy tee and the peppermint toothpaste I lent her when we were in the Ladies'. "My dad says I've spoiled her, he says she's no good."

One last gulp and Willa stops. She looks straight at me now, like she's forgotten I'm the kid who's been counting her onion rings. Who's been laughing at all her mistakes. "He means it, Hazel."

"It's Hazmat," I tell her.

"Hazmat." She says my handle over to herself, as if she's memorizing something important. "He always does what he says, Hazmat."

"So does *my* dad." I look across the picnic table, and my father stands up.

He walks over to our side of the table. He doesn't touch Willa, just stands beside her and talks slowly, gently—as if she were a trapped animal, as if he didn't want to startle her. "Do you have any relatives back home?"

Willa looks up at him, shakes her head. "My father has a brother, but they're not speaking on account of he's in jail."

Now it's Daddy's turn to shake his head. It sounds as if having a family like Willa's is worse than having no one at all. He reminds her that we've got two more days 'til we reach Denver, that she's got time to think things over. "If you want," he says, "we'll turn around after the drop-off, and we'll drive you back to Maryland. We'll go off the books, and we'll stay with you 'til we find you protection."

"And Sasha, too," I promise.

Willa just nods. I take this as a "yes," and as we head back to the truck, she follows me, hauling herself into the cab when I open the door. After she's settled in the bottom bunk and we're locked in for the night, I lean down from my perch above her.

"Think it over?" I whisper.

She doesn't say anything, and it's too dark to be sure. But I think maybe she nods again. I hope so.

STAR CRAZY

This morning, Willa is trying harder. She behaves herself at the warehouse, and we load our shipment in record time. After, while my father is getting gas, she shows me her collection of movie magazines, and she talks to me like I'm just another girl, not some baby she needs to entertain. "This here?" she says, pointing to a page where a teenager with a red stripe in her hair and a leather jacket is laughing in front of the Eiffel Tower. "This is the set for Nora Pearson's newest movie." She studies the page, like Nora Pearson is the most gifted star in the world and you can absorb acting tips just by looking at her picture. "She's from Maryland, right near where I live." She stops, corrects herself. "Used to live, I mean."

"I like her hair." I study the photo and the pouting teen who isn't at all impressed that she's standing in front of "La Tour Eiffel," as the videos in our unit on France called it. Daddy said my accent was horrible, but my paragraph on the tower's role in history was A-plus.

Willa can't stop staring at that photo. I guess she's a really serious fan. "You know how Nora got her start?" she asks me. Then, because she can see I don't, she tells me. "She was just messing around, busting a few steps on JimJam, when—"

"JimJam?" Maybe the difference between fifteen and eleven is too big for me to pretend I know this stuff. Or maybe since Daddy and I never use our cell phones for anything but staying on the right road, I can't possibly keep up. "What's that?"

Willa looks at me as if I'm from another planet, then scrounges in her backpack and takes out the saddest-looking cell phone I've ever seen. Its screen is cracked in three different places, and it has a fuzzy cover that clearly once, well, *covered*, but now just hangs by a thread. "I'm running out of minutes, so I can't stay on long." She thumbs through screens like a majorette twirling a baton, finds what she wants, and shows me a site where kids are doing thirty-second videos—it's silly stuff, funny stuff, and yes, I laugh.

But then I stop laughing and start thinking. Can someone really get movie makers' attention this way? "Grown-ups watch this?" I ask.

"You bet they do." Willa lets one video after another play across her broken screen, which makes it look as if everyone is dancing underwater. "Producers and directors, big companies—they're all looking for new talent this way." She rifles through more videos 'til she finds what she's been looking for. It's just as short as the others, but she plays it over and over, so I finally figure it out.

"That's *you!*" I watch a girl with grape-colored lipstick that makes her mouth look like a circus clown's and earrings as big as chandeliers.

She's wiggling and laughing and pretending to smoke a giant cigarette in a long black holder. She's trying really, really hard to look older than she is.

"Wow!" I say.

"I know." She looks at the video about six more times before she puts her phone away. "This is my third Jam, and I keep getting more likes with each one." She points proudly to the little red hearts under her video.

I study those hearts. Each one is someone who's watched Willa dance. And one of those someones could be a movie director. A movie director who could make a movie about Leonardo and Dad and me. A movie that could make everyone understand how important truckers are!

By the time my father has fueled up and brought the truck around, I've got a plan. A plan to make sure Leonardo and trucks everywhere get Hollywood's attention again. "They don't make movies like that anymore." That's what Daddy said after we watched *Smokey and the Bandit* in Iowa City. Well, it's about time somebody did!

I have to wait for just the right moment—a moment Willa and I are alone in the truck. It's not until we stop for lunch in South Bend off 90 that I get the chance. The three of us are standing in the endless line at Express Burgers, which is definitely not named for the speed of its service. "Oh no!" I say, as if I hadn't worked out this whole clever scheme in advance. "I'm glad I remembered. Today is Yoly's birthday!"

"Yoly?" Daddy asks.

"You know, Yolanda? My truck buddy?"

Daddy nods.

"I need to send her a birthday eCard before she gets to Canyon Ranch for her 'Day of Beauty.'"

"Beauty?" Daddy is already confused. "Is this the same Yolanda who hauls for Fast Trak?"

"It's a present from her husband. They're going to stay in a fancy hotel with a spa, and she gets to spend the whole day doing massages and mudpacks."

"Oooooh!" Willa says. "I went to a sleepover once. We all wore apple and honey masks overnight."

"Cool." I point back to the parking lot, then send Willa a super-strong psychic mind lock. "Run back to the truck with me, and you can tell me every drippy detail." I turn to my father. "Is that okay, Daddy? You know we both want supers with fries, right?"

Daddy nods again. I think he's glad to see me trying to be friends.

I guess the mind lock worked, because Willa's right behind me when we head for the lot and Leonardo. I turn back and wave my keys at my father before he can remind me. "Yep," I tell him. "I'll lock up 'til you come."

As soon as we find the truck, I get Willa to give me a boost up so

I can sit on Leonardo's hood. Then I ask her to shoot my new video for JimJam!

Willa has no idea what I've got in mind. And she *really* doesn't want to use up her storage space. "Pretty soon I won't even be able to text," she tells me. "Why can't we use your dad's phone?"

I launch into one of Daddy's finger-counting routines. "A," I say, holding up my pointer, "I don't want him to know about this." Now my middle finger. "B, you're the only one who knows how to get my video on that jimmy jammy site of yours . . ." Finally, my ring finger. "And C, I'll buy you a phone with a trillion terabytes of storage—just as soon as my dad and I are famous."

So that last one needs some explaining, and I don't have much time before Daddy comes back with our food. I tell Willa how robo-trucks are destroying trucking and how I need to save it. *Fast.* I also tell her about how often I've dreamed of driving my own rig someday. How I've studied cab designs and grill guards and lots and lots of hood ornaments. Now I push myself up to a standing position at the end of the hood and strike a ballet pose. (Well, as close as I can get in sneakers and jeans.) I don't wiggle like Willa did in her video, but I laugh and shift into another pose right away.

Willa giggles.

"That's perfect," she says. And she starts shooting.

I remember all the shiny chrome hood toppers I've seen, and I don't know if I'm "busting moves," but it's fun to act them all out. To stand on my tiptoes and throw my arms out behind me as if Leonardo is sporting a life-sized flying eagle on his hood instead of the tiny one that actually decorates the top of his grill. Or to crouch down and arch my back like an angry cat. I move quickly, changing from one pose to another. I announce each, just in case my posture alone doesn't make things clear. "Hissing cobra," I announce, or "Snappy alligator." I'm a butterfly one second, a rocket launching into space the next.

That rocket pose? It's going fine until Willa suggests I should take off for real. "Jump from the hood for a grand finale," she yells. "I'll try to get a freeze frame on the way down."

I think about the end of my video—I'll be in mid-leap, my knees bent and my arms wide against a background of clouds, like all the people in ads who are leaping for joy over soft drinks and doughnuts and beer. It'll be terrific!

It requires extra juice to get airborne. Maybe a bit too much juice, as it turns out. When I lift off, my flight plan is to land beside Leonardo's right front tires . . . *on my feet.* Instead, when Daddy arrives with two big Express Burger bags, Willa is laughing hysterically and I'm sitting on the asphalt, wondering why my head is a tossed salad and I can't feel my toes.

"Girls?" Daddy puts the bags down, crouches beside me. For the next half hour, in between bites of his burger and fries, my father keeps checking in. He asks how my head feels, double-checks the Band-Aid he got out of our medical kit for the cut on my ankle, and wonders what on earth I was doing on the hood.

"I told you, Daddy," I explain. "Willa is helping me choose my favorite hood ornament." I don't mind repeating this again and again, since it's not really a lie. "You know, for when I have my own truck?"

Willa pitches right in and helps distract him before he can ask more questions. "I personally love the Ballerina," she tells Daddy, reenacting my pose. "But the Eagle is a close second. What do you think?" She lets her wing arms float behind her, and bingo! Daddy can't help laughing. (Sometimes even an annoying non-sister can come in pretty handy.)

Later, when Willa and I are taking our soggy plates and cups to the trash can, my swollen ankle forces me to drag behind her. "Are you sure," I ask, "this is how Nora Pearson got her start?"

"Of course!" Willa explains. "If it wasn't for JimJam, that big company would never have started making *Nora* nail polish and *Nora* cologne." She sounds almost as proud as if she had *her* own nail polish. "And if it wasn't for how many of her fans bought that perfume, Nora would never have gotten an audition for her first film."

"*Audition?*" My ankle is throbbing, and I'm pretty sorry I let Willa talk me into that high dive off Leonardo.

"So wait," I say. "It was the *audition* that changed her life. If Nora couldn't act, she wouldn't have gotten the part, right?"

"Well, duh," Willa admits. "But those videos got her noticed."

I sigh. *Hazel, a Trucker's Fragrance* isn't my idea of success. I drop my share of our trash in the mesh basket, and Willa and I head back toward the truck. "You'll see," Willa promises. "As soon as I get more data, I'll post your video. I'll come up with some great music to put behind those wild moves of yours." She grins. "You might get almost as many followers as me!"

When Willa reaches Dad, he's hunkered down checking some grease spots under the cab, but our hitcher seems more interested in something at the end of Leonardo's trailer.

By the time I've caught up to her, Willa has spotted a flatbed parked behind us. Sure enough, she's already chatting with the driver: "Gee," she says, "I wish my dad had a truck like this." That's the *exact same thing* she told my father right before she hitched a ride with us. Only her next ride might not be with someone she'd be nearly as safe with. My stomach tightens, and I decide not to let her out of my sight.

The day is warming up fast, and my father tells us he'll meet us back on the picnic benches. I'd like to suggest we treat Willa to a shower, but something tells me we'd better hit the road fast. So when she says she needs to go to the bathroom, I say I need to go, too.

The two of us head into the Ladies', but only one of us comes out.

"Where's Willa?" Daddy asks when I join him. He sounds worried. Maybe he heard Willa and the truck driver, too?

I tell him I stayed right beside her the whole time and even used the booth next to hers. But then Willa said she "had her monthly" and that I should go tell my father we'll have to wait a while.

Daddy looks at me, and I look at him. "What's a 'monthly'?" I ask.

I've seen my father look worried before. And I've seen him look embarrassed. But now? He looks worried and embarrassed at the same time.

"We're doing a unit on that next month," he tells me. He starts walking back toward the restrooms. "Right now, though? You've got to go find Willa."

I run back to the Ladies' and make a total fool of myself. I race up and down the rows of stalls calling Willa's name, opening every door. But it takes me only two minutes to realize she isn't there.

When I tell Daddy, we both sprint toward the parking lot, but it's too late. The flatbed is just pulling out, and my father curses when the truck disappears behind the hedge that runs around the rest stop. "I didn't even get his goddamned plate!"

Daddy almost never swears, so I know he's really mad at himself. We both shade our eyes, staring into the fierce new sun. But the glare's too much for us, and we can't pick out the truck in the rush of traffic on the other side of the hedge.

"Wish we still had that CB," Daddy says.

I used to love it when Daddy got on that little radio. I liked the funny handles the drivers used, and the way they got all excited about stuff just like they were kids on walkie-talkies. Daddy's CB name was "The Prof," and he said if I didn't like "Hazmat," I could pick a handle of my own. But before I got the chance, the potty mouths ruined everything.

Back in the truck, neither of us feels much like talking. I'm wondering what it would be like to have a father you're afraid of. I'm picturing Willa in that truck, talking to the driver, lying and joking and feeling scared inside.

We've pulled out of the lot and onto the highway when I find the movie magazines. They've been left on the bottom bunk, along with a note. I read it to Daddy as we start the last haul to Denver:

Hazel

These are for yu on account of yu like them. I need to travel lite plus I read them all anyways.

Peas Out,

Willamette

Reading this brings back the panic of watching that truck take off. The note is written on a napkin; the writing is a weird, sloppy blend of print and script. Either way, it proves one thing: Willa knew she was going to take off. She didn't just find that driver; she went looking for a ride. Away from us. *Why?*

"Daddy?" I don't exactly know how to ask the question, but my father reads my mind.

"I guess if people you love have let you down," he says, "it's hard to trust anyone else."

Now I ask a question I *know* he can't answer, but I have to ask it anyway. "Will she be all right?"

My father shakes his head. "I don't know, Haz," he tells me. He's watching the road because he has to, but he's doing that halfway thing he does when he wants to look at me, too. "I hope so." He swallows hard, touches his mirror without adjusting it. "I hope I didn't scare her off."

"You were trying to help," I say.

"Maybe I pushed too hard."

"Daddy?"

I think my father is still thinking about pushing too hard. He doesn't answer, and I'm not sure he's heard me. "Do you remember what that flatbed was hauling?"

"It looked like sewer pipes to me."

I get a pencil and a tiny notebook out of the case in the glove compartment. I write down *sewer pipes*. "What color was it?"

"The truck?" My father shakes his head again. "I wish it had been turquoise or orange or something easy to spot," he says. "I'm afraid it was plain old keep-on-trucking, mud-spattered red."

I write that down, too, even the part about mud. "I think we need to keep watching for it," I tell him. "Every time we stop to eat or fill up, you know?"

"You bet we will," Daddy says. "But Haz, you need to know that if someone doesn't want to be found, it's pretty easy to disappear on the road."

"I know." I prop the notebook in the middle of our dash. "I think we should be on the lookout anyway, okay?"

TAKING NOTES

The magazines are slipped into three plastic folders to protect them. There must be thirty at least. The type is rubbed off on some pages, but you can see Willa tried to take good care of them. There are no bent pages and no ads ripped out. Once we've got the GPS set, I start leafing through them. I'm not sure what I'm looking for, unless it's pieces of Willa—articles I think she might have read, celebrities she might have loved.

An hour later? I've learned there are lots of kids who are homeschooled just like me. Only they study at the studio and they work in films. I've read dozens of features about musicals that have been turned into movies, and even more stories about how monster, horror, and alien films are shot. But you know what I *haven't* read about? Movies about drivers like Daddy.

It's like the lady at the truck stop told us—Hollywood stopped making trucker movies after the classic films that Daddy and I have watched over and over—*Smokey and the Bandit, Big Trouble in Little China, Convoy,* even *Flatbed Annie and Sweetie Pie* (which I made Daddy watch because it's about two lady truckers). Those movies were made thirty years before I was even born, and I guess the film capital of the world agrees with Daddy and Red and all the other drivers who keep saying no one cares about trucking anymore.

I've been through every last article in the complete Willamette Film Magazine Collection, and I've found stories about directors shooting movies that star actors playing doctors, nurses, nuns, and firemen. There are new films where a clown or businessman or even a criminal takes center stage. There are plans for biopics about famous actors, comics, and ordinary nobodies who get lost trying to climb a mountain, live with five hundred cats, or go crazy and turn into serial killers.

But the men and women who get carpal tunnel from wrestling with mega-steering wheels? The ones who watch the whole country fly by their windows on the way to delivering your breakfast cereal? The ones who get docked if it isn't there on time? Or if they cheat on their sleep to make sure it is? There's been only *one* big film about them in the last twenty years. It was also made before I was born, and it's a documentary, "educational," but not very dramatic. The article about it in *Screen Gems* says it's full of real-life interviews with drivers from all over the country. But it also says, "This film makes up in numbers what it lacks in narrative." That means it doesn't have a story. Which means it can't give moviegoers what *my* script will—a hold-your-breath, can't-take-your-eyes-off-the-screen *adventure*!

So now I'm circling the name of every director I can find. I'm pretty sure these magazines were Willa's way of saying thank you. But I don't think she had any idea of what a gift she was giving us. Because I'm going to write all those studio bigwigs about Daddy and me! If we aren't biopic material, who is? Every issue of *Screen Dreams* and *Inside Hollywood* is full of ads for companies that will help you pitch your movie to Hollywood: Pitch Perfect. Script Star. Story Fixers. They all want to help you get famous quick. One of them will even send you a free pitch letter sample if you give them your email address. Easy peasy.

Of course, I have to do my part, too. Even if Willa remembers to upload my imitations of hood ornaments, a crazy half-minute video isn't a ticket to stardom. I need to tell our story, Daddy's and mine. So I'm going to write down every move we make, describe all the people we meet and the places we go. If a movie about what my father does every single day doesn't change people's minds about driverless trucks, nothing will. Think about it: Could a computerized trailer stop and change a tire for a stranded four-wheeler? Would it save lives by giving CPR at the scene of an accident? Can a driverless truck repair its own engine in the middle of the night? Chain up its tires in a mountain snowstorm? Wave to twenty-six kids, one at a time, in a passing school bus?

"Hazmat?" Daddy's at a stoplight, and he's watching me scribble in the magazines. "What are you doing?"

I don't ever lie to my father. (Today really *is* Yoly Mendez's birthday.) But I don't always tell him the truth, either. (I would never forget my road buddy's birthday, and I already sent her an eCard last night.) "Taking notes," I say.

"Notes?"

"Yeah." I smile my best, most adorable smile. "Willa isn't the only one who'd like to go to Hollywood." I close the magazines, so he can't see what I've circled. "There are lots of studios we can visit," I tell him. "Universal, Paramount, Warner Brothers—"

"Okay." Daddy's nodding, thinking it over. "We could ask Mazen to bid a job in L.A." He grins at me, holds out one hand for a high five.

He's not looking for one of our super-duper, nine-part Ritual High Fives. So we just slap hands and I'm back to plotting. The more I think about it, the more I'm sure our movie will be a blockbuster. I'm going to call it *Wheels of Fire*, and it will have everything— romance, tears, adventure, heroism. The opening scene will be the kissy, romantic part, when my father and Mom get married. He's a handsome professor, and she's his beautiful graduate student. Then I come along.

Daddy throws me right out of my technicolor daydream. He sounds really happy and proud of himself. "If you want to go to Hollywood," he tells me, "then that's what we'll do." He's been planning, just like me. But instead of a mega movie deal, he's high on our next homeschooling adventure. "On the drive out, we'll study the history of film. Then when we get to town, we can do a unit on acting, maybe work as extras on a couple of movie sets."

I look appropriately excited, then I pick up the last folder of Willa's magazines. I don't care what she says; I'm not going to just sit around and wait to go viral on JimJam. Besides, now that she's run off, she probably has lots more to think about than that video we made. For a second, I get a bad case of worried. Where *is* Willa, anyway? I wish you could put a bubble around people who leave you, not to keep them with you, but just to keep them safe.

Even without the magazines in this folder, I've already got ten directors' names from the other two. I'll pitch them all. I'll send them the whole story. I'll get the sad part over with first, the part where Mom's blood and my blood get mixed up and it makes her sick. I'm premature, and the hospital says I'll have to stay in an incubator for a month. I'm so small that my parents can't even hold me. Mom's already feeling horrible. But she makes the nurses push her chair to where she can touch me through a tiny flexi tube . . .

"Before we worry about movies, though"—Daddy clears his throat and uses his "announcement" voice—"we're going to do a unit on human reproduction."

"Okay." I'm not really listening now. I'm thinking about how the doctors couldn't keep Mom alive. About how my father stopped wanting to do much of anything after she died. How he left me with Serena and Mazen while he figured out how to stop drinking and start loving again.

"Hazel?" We're stopped at another traffic light. Daddy's turned away from the wheel to look at me. Waiting.

"Human what?" I say.

"Listen." He looks back at the road when the light changes, and now that he's talking to the highway instead of me, his words come faster, more easily. "You know where babies come from, right?"

"Dad!" I put down the pencil and the magazines. "I'm eleven years old, for crying out loud." Sometimes my father forgets that eleven is plenty old enough to know lots of things. How to cook awesome cheese-and-pepper omelettes. How to find parking for a forty-ton truck. Why stars fall. Where babies come— "Wait." Now he's got my attention. "Are we going to study *S-E-X*?"

"*You're* going to, well . . . discover a bit more about . . . some of the finer . . . Oh, for God's sake, Hazel! It's time you learned what a monthly is."

THE GREAT AMERICAN ~~NOVEL~~ MOVIE

I've decided to write down everything that might go into our movie, and that means I'll need a lot more space than the itty-bitty notebook I put on the dash to help us find Willa. The trouble is, I want to wait until we sell *Wheels of Fire* to Hollywood before I tell Daddy what I'm doing. So I have to be pretty sneaky about slipping a brand-new spiral notebook in with the water and sodas I bring back from our fuel stop.

I wish I'd chosen another color, because my father spots the splashy purple notebook while we're putting our root beers and orange Nehis in the mini fridge. "What's this?" asks Inspector Eagle Eye.

"Remember that journal you had me start for our creative writing unit last summer?"

The Inspector nods.

"It's almost full."

"That's great, Hazmat." The Inspector loves it when I take on what he calls "independent learning." "I'm glad you're inspired." He grins and suggests we go back for some pens and colored markers.

"Who knows?" As we head back into Presto Pick, I'm feeling a little guilty, but my father is plainly pumped. "Maybe you'll write the Great American Novel?" he says. "It's about time *somebody* did!"

Once we're on the road again, I take out the new notebook and write THE GREAT AMERICAN NOVEL on the cover. After I'm sure Daddy's had a chance to read my extra-large print, I open it up and start hatching. "Coming soon to a theater near you, this story will take you places you've never been." That's a big promise, but it's true. And I'm going to send it to all ten of the Hollywood directors whose names I've found in Willa's zines.

The thing is, after the sad part where we lose Mom, I'm not sure where to start the action, the scenes that show how super heroic truckers are. That's because for the first few years of my life, it was Mazen and Serena who mostly took care of me. Except for those maybe-made-up memories from the hospital? What I remember first and best is Serena's voice putting me to sleep and the way the sun filled her and Mazen's house every morning, like syrup poured all over a new day.

Sure, Daddy stopped by back then, but he was more a big, handsome visitor than someone I knew really well. Serena says he was "putting the pieces back together" all that time, and I guess that's true, because even after I learned to talk, he didn't ever say much to me. Mostly? He would hand me a stuffed toy or a doll that spoke, and then he'd kneel down and just look into my eyes. It felt like he'd lost something in there he was looking for, but I don't think he ever found it. Because he'd just stand up again, sigh, and then he and Mazen would go sit in the den and talk all low and rumbly 'til Serena put me to bed.

We had bedtime all worked out, Serena and me. First, she'd read a book. And after all the fun and exciting parts, she'd read a sentence with words that got slow and winding and finally finished with *THE END*. I double-, triple-, quadruple-hated to hear those words. "More!" I'd beg. And poor Serena would turn back to the beginning of the book and start all over. "No!" I'd say. "More!"

She didn't get it. She kept trying to start the story all over, but that wasn't what I wanted. So after she had brushed the tears and hair away from my face, after she'd told me "Sleep tight, don't let the bedbugs bite," I took care of things myself. I lay in bed and added on more and more story, more and more adventures. And every night I fell asleep without ever coming to *THE END*.

But that's all backstory, right? It could come after the kiss and the credits, after the hospital scene and some sad, spun-sugar music. My movie will really get interesting, though, when Daddy and I start trucking. There will be scenes that nearly stop your heart, like the time my father saved another trucker's life by nosing his runaway twenty-four-wheeler onto an escape ramp. Or the time a minivan full of teenagers coming onto a highway tried to play chicken with us. They forgot, like most four-wheelers do, that they weighed only a few thousand pounds and that, fully loaded, we weigh more than sixty thousand. Daddy saved their lives, too, and all he had to show for it were smoking brakes.

Now I just have to wait for something really big to happen, something that will be our climax—that's the point in a story where the hero (Daddy) and the heroine (me) have their greatest adventure of all. The one that will convince everyone in the audience that a computerized road drone is no match for a brave, smart, flesh-and-blood trucker. The one that will mean Daddy can keep on trucking and we never have to give up hauling.

The trouble with climaxes, of course, is that they involve dangerous, scary action. They have to make the audience breathe faster and wonder if we're going to make it. But with Daddy being one of the fastest-thinking drivers on the road, and me being a pretty good navigator, and both of us working for the best boss on the planet, there's not too much suspense involved. I mean, DUH. Of course we're going to make it.

"Hazmat?"

I cover up my notes and realize we've pulled into the last stop before Denver. We've made really good time. I stash my notebook under the seat. "Are we off the clock?" I ask Daddy.

He smiles his off-the-clock smile. "Yep."

"Can we take a look around?" I scan the parking lot, see the store, the restaurant. "You know, just in case she's here?"

"Willa?" Daddy hasn't had *The Great American Trucker Movie* to keep him busy. I'll bet he's been thinking about her, too.

I nod, look toward the restrooms. "You do the coffee shop, I'll do the Ladies'. Okay?"

Of course, I know better. But I look in every stall anyway. No Willa. On my way back to the truck, I see a sign with a cartoon man lifting weights above a door beside the coffee shop. I meet Daddy as he's coming out of Joe to Go. He doesn't need to tell me Willa wasn't in there eating everything she could get her hands on. He just shakes his head.

"Then can we work out?" I love the truck stops with gyms, and I point to the sign next door. There are perspiration drops coming off the cartoon man, but he's wearing a big smile just the same.

"Loser of the decathlon buys dinner!" Daddy opens the door under the sweating man, and we find a small workout room with a window overlooking the parking lot. My father and me? We do this thing in gyms, at least when they're not too crowded: we each pick a piece of equipment, then pretend to be a bodybuilder demonstrating its proper use. We do ten reps of a made-up exercise, and whoever doesn't laugh wins. Daddy does this amazing Arnold Schwarzenegger imitation, so I mostly lose.

There's no one else here. It's warm and one of the windows is open, which is a good thing because the whole place smells of sweat and beer. Both weight benches are stained, and the treadmill has a dark path worn straight down the middle. I head for the elliptical, so Daddy has to settle for a bike. I flex my fake muscles and start stepping. "You think you've got the body of a champ?" I ask in as deep a voice as I can manage.

My father leans against his bike, pretending I'm a fitness expert and he's hanging on my every word.

It feels good to forget about lonely runaways and robo-trucks. I fall right into my role, a trainer with a mission: "You don't know what fitness is 'til you've tried working out *my* way," I tell him. Then suddenly I jump up and turn around so I'm facing the wrong way on the machine. I do a few steps but stop before I lose my balance. "My way is BACKWARD," I announce, spreading my arms and nearly toppling off. "You'll stay trim and slim and light and lean," I promise, grabbing the handles again. "And best of all, you'll be able to wave goodbye to all that flab!" I wave at my father, who starts to smile, but then covers his mouth.

I'm close, so I push my advantage. "You call those little biceps muscles?" I point at Daddy and laugh, hoping he will, too. "Why, a mouse has bigger muscles! A little, bitty . . ."

I stop. And listen. I'm sure I heard something just now, something crazy. It was right outside the window behind me.

Daddy's listening, too. We forget about our game and move toward the open window. The noise has stopped, but when we're up close, we hear it again.

A long, miserable wail. We look at each other, too surprised to say a word. And the sound keeps coming. The window looks out on a horseshoe pit, then on row after row of vans and trucks. But right underneath the window, where we can't see, the wail grows.

Somebody is crying, and they just can't stop.

OH, BABY!

When we race outside and walk toward the crying, it's not hard to figure out where it's coming from. And *who* it's coming from. What we find is just what it sounds like—a real live, very unhappy baby. Someone has tried to make it comfortable, or as comfortable as you can be, alone outside a truck stop on a major highway. Blankets have been folded tightly around it, and it's been set inside a cardboard box nested deep in the forsythia under the weight room's bay window. If you don't count the screaming and the red cheeks, it looks like one of the babies on the labels of strained peaches or bananas.

I can't stop staring. I've never seen anything like this in real life. Its tiny face is actually purple, not red now, and its fists have fought their way out of the blankets and are rubbing its ears and mouth. It's hiccupping in between sobs, choking with misery. I feel my own fists balling up just like the baby's, until I figure out what to do with them. I stoop down and try to pick up the box, but I'm afraid I'll drop it. "Daddy," I say, not looking behind me, just knowing he's there. "What can we do?"

He bends down next to me, then helps lift the box up slowly, slowly. Even so, the baby startles and stops crying for a moment. I talk into the quiet space, speaking as softly as I can. "It's okay," I tell it. "You're going to be okay."

For a split second, that little baby looks at me and everything goes still. I think it understood me, but then the crying starts up again, harder than before. Daddy is peering into the box, too. "Is she hungry?" I ask him. (I know the baby's a girl now. Her pink hands, her eyes, I just know.) I pull my father toward the restaurant. "Shouldn't we get her something to eat?"

Daddy stops, puts the box on a bench, and lifts the baby out, holding her against his chest. "I remember Serena doing this with you when we brought you home," he tells me. The crying may not actually be any softer now, but it's muffled against his shirt. He pats the baby's back through the blanket. "She'll need formula, not food," he says. (Daddy thinks she's a girl, too.)

"Eleven years ago, when Maze drove me home with you?" Daddy's jiggling the baby up and down now, and I guess he knows what he's doing, because suddenly she burps. "I was not exactly a candidate for Father of the Year." The baby's loud burp has surprised even her, and she turns her head on his chest so that she and I are staring at each other again.

"It's okay," I say. Daddy has told me how it was hard to look at me when I was a baby and Mom had just died. "You made up for it later."

"Hmmm." He nods, but he doesn't sound like he believes me. "It wasn't you, you know that, right?" The baby is crying again, and Daddy heads for the Hasty-Mart. "I just couldn't bear to look at a miniature Glory. A helpless, needy new soul who'd filched her mother's eyes and nose."

I reach up and hook my hand over his arm, the one that's under the baby's legs. "Filched?" I ask.

"Stole," Daddy explains. "But of course you didn't. She gave them to you."

I don't say it: how I wish she could have given me lots more, how I wish there had been time. I know my father wishes the same thing. He's told me before how he ran away. How he left me behind with Serena and Mazen. How he did a lot of crying. And a lot of drinking. How he didn't come back until he was sure he could really, truly be a dad.

The baby is really wailing now. And we're lucky there's a sympathetic woman at the checkout counter. She rounds up diapers and wipes, then, even though Hasty-Mart doesn't stock formula, she sends a kid who works for her to pick up a carton from the Walmart down the highway. When he gets back, she grabs up the bag and leads us into the employees' lounge. She changes the baby on a table beside a sign that reminds us to wash our hands before returning to work. The whole room smells of disinfectant and cigarettes.

"That," she announces a few minutes later, taping a fresh diaper around the baby's legs, "is all she needed." Then she hands the baby, who is suddenly quieter and definitely a girl, to me.

To me! It's like she thinks I've done this before! Or maybe she doesn't, because she helps me cradle the baby, then makes me sit on the bench to hold her in my lap. "She's cute when she's not crying," I say. That baby is staring at me now. It feels like her eyes are Velcroed to mine, as if everything she needs is here, looking down at her.

When I was this size, of course, I was mostly staring at Serena. And Daddy was studying the bottom of a glass. He says he went to AA meetings, but only because Mazen told him they wouldn't take care of me unless he did.

He says it finally came down to one thing, one person who made him stop drinking. It was baby Hazel, wiggling like a puppy whenever he came to the house. For a while, though, he didn't get it. He thought I was wiggling because he brought toys with him. He thought all I needed was a talking doll who looked at me from under her big, lazy lashes and said things without opening her mouth: *Hi, my name is Kathy. Will you be my friend? . . . It's fun to learn. . . . Let's learn about colors. . . . Hi, my name is Kathy. . . .*

It turns out, I needed a lot more. I needed the way we've learned the constellations and the continents together; the way we've zigzagged across this country and made a home that's bigger and wider than any house you could ever build.

By the time the security guard for the truck stop shows up, I've handed the baby to Daddy and I'm helping Ivy, the checker, heat up a bottle. It turns out she has five children at home—no wonder she knows her way around diapers and formula! Daddy tells the guard where and how we found the baby, and the guard tells us this is a first. "We get lost dogs, course," he says. "And once someone left an alligator in the restroom. But babies?"

"So, what happens now?" I ask. "Do we call the police?"

We do, and they send a social worker named Mrs. Spencer. That's how she introduces herself. She shakes everyone's hands. "I'm Mrs. Spencer," she says, "from Child Welfare." She's okay, but she doesn't seem to know as much about kids as Ivy does. And when she picks up the baby, I can tell she's a little nervous. "Every state has a Safe Haven law," she tells Daddy. "There are places you can leave a baby and not be charged." She studies the infant in her arms. She doesn't smile, just shakes her head.

"Then why would someone leave her"—I look around us, at the oily tablecloth, the filthy broom jammed into a corner—"here?"

"Some people don't know any better," the caseworker says. "And others don't want to answer questions."

I can't stop looking at the baby in her arms. She's had almost a whole bottle of formula and she's nearly asleep, but one hand curls shut, then opens slowly. Her tiny nails glisten like fairy glass. Daddy's looking at her, too. Like he's taking notes. Like there'll be a quiz. Like he doesn't want to forget one single solitary hair on her fuzzy, nearly bald head.

I ask it without taking my eyes off the baby: "Could we, you know, keep her?"

"I have to take her to the hospital, honey," the woman from Child Welfare says. "She needs to get a full medical workup. Then she'll go into the foster-care system." Mrs. Spencer seems a little better with older kids than babies. I like the way she looks right at me when she talks to me. Almost like I'm another adult.

"Foster?"

"We pay people to take care of her, right along with their own family. Until someone adopts her for good."

"Oh." There's a lump in my throat when I look back down at the baby. I can see a web of pale veins in her eyelids. And I notice there's a wet spot on her collar, where she's drooled onto her onesie.

Once Mrs. Sharon Justa Spencer (that's the full name on the card she leaves with us) has driven off with the baby, Daddy asks me if I want to play a game of horseshoes before dinner. He even tells me he'll spot me a ten-foot advantage. Normally? I'd be all over the chance to beat him. But not tonight. Who needs to beat someone who's feeling the same hole in the heart you are?

"She wasn't like a doll at all," I say as we cut back through the weight room, then head outside again to the restaurant.

"No," he tells me. "She wasn't." You can bet he's worrying about lost babies, too. And left-behind kids. He squeezes my hand.

"I was thinking of a name," I say. "You know, for if they let us keep her."

"It doesn't work that way, Hazel. You understand that, don't you?" He stops, turns me around to face him. "It's not the same as a lost dog or cat, right?"

"I know." The sunset is making me squint, so I hope he doesn't think I'm crying. "But I'm going to use it when I think about her."

He doesn't ask what the name is. He just waits.

I shade my eyes with one hand to look up at him. "It's Denver," I say. "I'm going to call her Denver."

JUST A TRIM

"**I** need a haircut." I'm looking in the mirror on my visor, and it's true. The kid who's looking back at me has bangs like a sheepdog and no eyebrows in sight. I remember the photo of Nora Pearson, the teenage actress Willa loves, the one with a buzz cut and red hair. She *did* look kind of nervy and cool, and I'm pretty sure she never has to push her hair out of her face to see where she's going.

"Let's wait 'til we get back to Chapel Hill," Daddy says. "Serena can do us both."

My father loves to do stuff the way we've always done it: our Secret High Five, our Good Night Ritual, even the way we trade fortune cookies when we order Chinese. Daddy calls this stuff "tradition," and I think having Serena stick us on top of two barstools while she sings and snips is definitely a tradition. But I've got something different in mind. Very different.

"I want an undercut," I announce. (And then I duck for cover.)

"A what?"

"It's sort of a pixie cut," I explain. "Only my head would be shaved on the sides."

"Shaved?"

I show him two pictures from Willa's magazines. He starts shaking his head before he's even looked at both of them. When he has, he stops the headshaking and narrows his eyes. "This is a joke," he asks me, "right?"

"Cissy Mendez," I read from the caption under the picture of a TV star with a bleached strip of hair on top of her otherwise bald head, "makes all A's at Hollywood High."

"Well, I've got an 'A' for *you*, missy." My father's wearing his Because-I'm-Your-Father face, so I'm pretty sure I know what's coming. "*Absolutely* not."

I play my winning card. "I'm asking Mom," I tell him. I put the magazines down and turn toward the green box on the dash, but Daddy puts his hand on mine.

"Don't drag your mother into this, Hazel." He looks so serious, I shut Cissy back up in the magazine. "This is between you and me."

We've spent an hour at this warehouse already. If we could unload the flooring we're hauling ourselves, things would go much faster. But warehouse rules here won't let us, and the dock crew are handling only a few trucks an hour. The line goes down the block. We're both tired of waiting, and yes, you're right, it probably wasn't the best time to mention a new hairstyle.

But honestly? There hasn't *been* a good time for mentioning much of anything lately, not since that social worker phoned last night to tell us that Denver's mom changed her mind and came back for her baby. We were eating dinner at the truck stop where we found her, and neither of us was particularly cheerful. Daddy told me I was too picky, and I told him he'd forgotten what good lasagna tastes like. When his cell went off, he didn't know who it was at first. Then, when he'd been on the phone a few minutes, I saw his whole face go hard. From his end of the conversation, I knew it had to be Mrs. Spencer, and from the way he sounded, I was afraid maybe something horrible had happened.

But then he told me that Denver was back with her own original mom. You'd think he'd be happy, but he wasn't. He got grumpy and snappy, and I don't mean like a cartoon dwarf. I mean like, when I asked how come you're allowed to give babies away and then take them back, he looked at me the way he looks at the guys at the weigh station who ask him to drive through the scales again.

"I thought you said it wasn't like a dog or a cat," I tried to explain.

"Maybe I was wrong," he said. "Maybe it's exactly the same as a dog or cat. Maybe the powers that be don't care who really wants her, who's not going to bring her back every time the wind changes."

Today isn't any better. The wait at the warehouse has made the heat hotter and Daddy's mood moodier. For the record? We're *both* sweaty and cranky, but one of us (guess who) is handling it with a lot more maturity than the other. So when my father tells me to leave him alone and start the next study unit, I decide my nose in a book beats dealing with Mr. Snap Your Head Off If You Even Hint that Maybe Sugar Isn't as Bad as Heatstroke and that Coca-Cola Used to Be Considered a Medicine.

I wrestle the cardboard mailer out of the glove compartment and slip out *New Body, New Self.* That's the name of the text and workbook we picked up at the Denver post office on the way here. I have Willa to thank for this—it wasn't 'til she used the word "monthly" that Daddy decided I didn't know enough about S-E-X. Thinking about Willa makes me sad, and I start wondering where that dirty red flatbed was headed. I remember how she asked if she could stay with us . . . and how she changed her mind.

I'm nearly as grumpy as my father by the time I force myself to focus on the new book. Plus, I have to say? There's nothing very sexy about the cover. It's dotted with purple and pink lady shapes of all colors and sizes, each with a white balloon-thing in their middle. And every balloon has two squash growing out of it. *Ewwww!*

I don't know if Daddy is still embarrassed about "monthly" or if he's just too hot and tired to go over the first chapter with me like we usually do. He doesn't even look up when I open the book. He acts like he's fascinated with something outside the window, even though what's there is what's been there for over an hour now—lots of other trucks waiting, same as we are. Still, I figure I might as well find out what all the fuss is about. So while Daddy stares, eyes front, at rows of eighteen-wheelers baking in the sun, I start reading.

I'm not too thrilled by what I learn out of the gate: "Your life is about to be transformed," the first page announces. "You are not a little girl anymore, and like every growing thing, you are changing each day." This is definitely not the best news for someone who has already decided to opt out of adulthood. "You are becoming a woman," I read, "who may one day have her own home and children. On the way from here to there, an exciting journey of discovery awaits."

I am very close to shutting this book. Fast and hard. My own home is not something I'm in the market for. Daddy and I already have one together, and I like it just fine, thank you very much. Mr. Grouch and life on the road are better than anyone else and a house with a foundation that's stuck in the ground, any day. (Except maybe the days of Thanksgiving and Christmas, which we always spend at Maze and Serena's.) But I decide to give my *New Self* one more chance: Puberty opens the door to womanhood. Whenever you walk through it, somewhere between the ages of nine (did they say "nine"? Is that a typo?) and sixteen, you'll have lots of questions: *Why do I have cramps? Why am I bleeding? Why do I feel so tired?* This book will help answer your questions and will serve as a guide throughout this wonderful time of transition.

"Cramps"? "Bleeding"? "*Wonderful*"? I read a few pages ahead now, but it's more like fast-forwarding a scary movie just to see how it ends.

What I figure out is that I could get my period anytime, anywhere. And there's nothing I can do to stop it. I'm pretty sure I don't want to read anymore, and lucky for me, the line for the unloading bays just got five rigs shorter. Which means I have to help Daddy get the paperwork ready on the shipment.

Plus I'll need to enter all the downtime in the log. I've got a special code I figured out for those columns—NUT! It stands for "Not us, them"—and I've been using it a lot lately. Between waiting in lines like this, accidents and construction on the road, loading, unloading, hurricanes, thunderstorms, tornadoes, and breakdowns (Leonardo has trouble starting in the cold, but then so do Daddy and I), it just got too hard to use separate columns for each kind of delay.

I'm working on the log in the truckers' waiting room when Daddy joins me *way too soon.* I study his face, which has gone from sulky to angry. "What happened?" I ask.

"First they tell me to drive to bay three, and next they ask me to get out of the truck. Then they charge us a lumper fee to unload it." He shakes his head, sighs into the seat next to mine. "Why should I have to pass that charge on to Maze? I mean, if suddenly they want their pallets stacked in ten rows of fifty," he grumbles, "that's their problem, not ours."

Frankly, I can't wait to dump this load, deliver the next, and then check in with Maze and Serena. It will be good to talk to someone who hasn't got a mile-high chip on their shoulder. And if you ask me?

That chip on Daddy's shoulder comes from hoping the same thing I was about Denver. I know he's a grown-up; I know he's told me a dozen times there's no way anyone would give a baby to people like us—people who don't have an address. Or beds with ruffles. Or a yard with a barbecue.

But I remember the way he looked at Denver when she was sleeping. I could almost hear the "what-ifs" in his head. And I'm pretty sure they were the same as the ones in mine: What if all the rules went away? What if the only thing that mattered was how much room you had in your heart, not the square footage of your cab? Without all the rights and wrongs, the can'ts and don'ts, wouldn't there be three of us on the road right now? Four, if you count Mom—who, by the way, I already told all about Denver. You know, just in case.

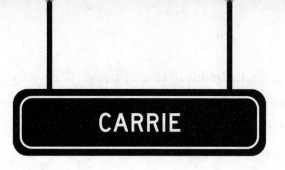

CARRIE

Unloading's done! Daddy's mood has lifted a bit, and the day is beginning to cool down. We celebrate the way we always do, with our synchronized, rapid-fire high five and a trip to the nearest soft-serve ice cream place. We're settled in with our cones when my father remembers how cranky he's been. "Hey," he says, handing me the cell. "Maybe it's time you had a chance to talk to someone who's not so prickly." Which isn't exactly the same as "I'm sorry I bit your head off for the last two days." But I'll take it.

It's time to check in with Maze, but I always get to do the Emo Report first if Serena answers. She does, so Daddy heads onto the highway while I give her an earful. I tell her about Willa and about Denver and how Heifitz is all alone now without Scheherazade. I'm talking so fast, she asks me to slow down and breathe. "I want to hear it all, Hazmatazz," she says. "So take your time."

I start over from the top. I'm just at the part where we find Denver when I realize we're hardly moving at all. I look up to find traffic crawling on both sides of 70. Daddy has had Leonardo in first gear so long, the engine sounds like it's panting. (He'd tell me that's low transmission fluid, but it sounds more like Leonardo is really, really fed up with stopping more than starting.)

"What's up?" I ask Daddy.

"What's happening?" Serena says in my ear.

"Looks like a plane crash," Daddy says. He's staring out my window at a field with a few farm buildings, six police cars, three ambulances, a fire truck, and a huge rectangle of yellow tape that's been set up right in the middle. I see people running and driving every which way, and yes, a big pile of metal and smoke way off in the distance. A pile that just might be an airplane that tried to land in the field. I tell Serena I'll call her back.

Since we're practically standing still, I have lots of time to gawk. I've only been on a plane once in my life, when Daddy and I had to leave Leonardo in Wyoming for a complete overhaul. I loved it, though, and once we took off, everything got quiet and slow, as if time had stopped. Honestly? It felt more like floating than flying. It's hard to imagine falling out of the sky as hard and as fast as that plane in the field must have.

"That's a little turboprop," my aero-junkie dad tells me. "Looks like a Piper."

My grandpa, who spent a lot of time in bed, used to watch planes out his window and tell Daddy all about them. "It only carries about six passengers."

All I can see is a lot of smoke and the last of the ambulances pulling out of the field onto the highway. "Are all of them . . . you know?" I swallow hard, look at Mom's box. "Dead?"

"I don't know." Daddy looks at me, then back at the heap of charred metal. There's one wing sticking up from it, and now I can see half the tail, too. "The airport's pretty close; if it happened just after takeoff . . ." He doesn't finish, just stares, his arms resting on the steering wheel he hasn't turned for miles.

I scrunch down low in my seat, sigh, think about calling Serena back. But then something in the middle of a pile of debris that's scattered out from the crash site, something only a few hundred feet from the highway, catches my eye. It looks like a battered laundry basket, *but it's moving*—all by itself, rocking back and forth in no wind at all. "Stop!" I yell, even though we already have. "I need to get out!"

"Why didn't you go the whole time we were at the warehouse?" Daddy asks.

I don't turn around, but I hear my father's question, the fear underneath it. I don't usually—okay, I never—leave a truck when it's running.

"Please! Please!" I smell a burnt-toast smell, spilled oil, too. I yank open the door and jump down from the cab. I know, I know. Getting out of our rig is the worst thing I could do *if* we were moving, or *if* there weren't hundreds of cars ahead and behind us, all of them cooling their heels—er, tires—same as we are.

"Hazel Denise Sampson!" Daddy is yelling after me. No *Hazel*. No *Hazmat*. The full whammy. He's really worried. But I keep right on running toward that laundry hamper.

Normally? I'd be looking behind me, concerned about the truck, about my father, and about what's going to happen when an object traveling at the speed of upset (Daddy) meets an object (me) that's now stopped in front of the jiggling, wiggling hamper. But all I can think about is that hamper and the way it's thumping and bumping against the ground.

Only it's not a hamper.

It's an animal carrier, and something inside is howling up a storm. There's a carry-on luggage tag attached to the top, and the sides are rocking back and forth, back and forth as if something were hurling itself from one end to the other.

I take a quick look behind me. Daddy has pulled over to the shoulder, which isn't much wider than Leonardo's cab. He's driven onto the grass, and now he gets out, slamming the door behind him.

It's pretty clear the carrier got thrown off the plane when it crashed and that whatever's inside is *alive*! And then I'm down on my knees, zipping open the flap in front. As soon as I do, a jet-black bundle of fear and fur leaps into my lap.

The ambulances have made it to the highway and are streaming down the eastbound lanes, their sirens ripping through the afternoon. But I don't even glance toward the street. All I care about right now is that formerly yowling black fur ball that's blinking its eyes in the space between my crossed legs.

The kitten stops its pitiful banshee wail for about two seconds, looks at me, and then tries to break my grip. But I hold tight and yes, the howling starts up again. And the trembling. It throws itself against me again and again. And then, suddenly for no reason I can figure out, it stops trying to get away.

It's as if someone has flipped a switch and turned on a tiny engine that's vibrating all through my legs and arms. By the time Daddy runs up behind me and touches my shoulder, the cat has nosed itself deep into my lap and it's purring. I'm patting it and crying at the same time, stroking the dark fur along its tiny backbone, top to bottom, over and over.

"It isn't a doll," I tell my father when he sits in the grass beside me. "And it isn't a baby, either."

"Nope," he agrees. He dangles one big finger above the kitten's head, and it rolls over on its back, batting at him with its paws. "It's a cat." He nods toward the carrier. "A very *lucky* cat."

No, we didn't name her Lucky. And yes, she's a girl, and no, her human owner wasn't so lucky. We stayed in town for two hours while Daddy checked on the crash. "No survivors." That's what the police told him when he called, and that's what the local radio station reported. Except of course they're wrong. There was a survivor, and we're calling her Carrie, after her carry-on bag.

The tag on her carrier doesn't list a name or address. It just has two words scrawled across the plastic surface: *Water Occasionally.*

"She sounds like a cactus," I tell Daddy. Then I remember our last orphan. "Should we take Carrie to the airport or an animal shelter? Do we need to report this to the police?"

"We could," Daddy says. "We could jump through hoops and fill out papers, and they'd put her in a cage and keep her there 'til we were done. And maybe, if all our i's were dotted and our t's crossed, we might get to adopt her."

I can tell my father's remembering Denver. And I can tell he's hoping this time, at least, caring is all that counts.

"*Might?*"

Daddy nods. "Or," he tells me, "we could skip all that and just take her with us right now." He smiles. I smile. And then we fist-bump. Carrie? She falls sound asleep as soon as I give her water in my cereal bowl and put her in a blanket nest on the bottom berth. I hope Mom lets Carrie's owners know their kitten has found a good home.

S-E-X

Feline survivor saved by caring trucker. That's how I'm going to pitch the scene for our movie. It may not be the climax, but it will be a highlight. I mean, it's one of the best adventures we've had.

Carrie has already learned how to climb up the ladder of sheets and towels I've tied to my top bunk. She and I slept there last night after the three of us made it through two four-cheese pizzas, one with half anchovies for Carrie. (We couldn't get any other seafood, and anchovies *are* fish, right?)

I hardly dared to move all night long. I didn't want to turn over or wiggle my feet, since that's where our new kitten had curled up— right in the middle of my legs. It must have seemed like a pretty safe space, complete with walls all around and a large body heater!

This morning? I wake up to a face wash. Only Carrie uses her tongue for a washcloth. First she licks the front of her own paw, then she licks my cheek. Then she licks her paw again and does my nose. She's very careful and slow, and you'll have to trust me. It feels sweet and tingly, like a fairy is massaging my face.

Plus, she's turning into a total road cat—after Daddy calls Maze and gives him the final figures on our drop-off, we go to breakfast, and Carrie guards the cab. (We leave the windows open the tiniest bit, so she can sniff the Great Outdoors but not escape into it.) When we get back, she cleans up all our leftovers, leaves most of the PURR-fect canned tuna we found at the store next to the diner, then jumps into my lap as soon as I start an audiobook. It's like she's been keeping track of the story and doesn't want to miss what happens next.

After we're underway, I pause the book to call Serena and tell her all about Carry-On Carrie, something Daddy completely forgot to include in his report to Maze. I try not to make our new pet sound too perfect, on account of I don't want Serena to make any adoption plans. She takes in strays all the time, perfect or not. At last count there was their old dog Shepherd, who's nearly blind now and basically lives under their dining room table, a doe who brings a new fawn to the backyard every season, two hutches full of rabbits, and a toad that lives in the flowerpot outside their front door.

"She's kind of cute," I concede when Serena asks. "I mean, if you like black cats." Our new team member is smack-dab in the middle of my lap while I'm talking, and I hope she forgives me for the "kind of." And for not mentioning her three white paws or the tip of her tail, which looks like it was dipped in vanilla ice cream. "But I don't think she'd make a very good house cat," I add. "She's gotten used to the truck."

"Well, I can't wait to meet her." Then Serena asks the same thing she always asks at the end of all our calls. "So," she says, "any touchy-feely?" She means is there any stuff I've been holding in and want to get out.

I'd sort of like to rant about moms who leave their kids. And then decide to take them back. But I figure with Daddy listening in, talking about Denver might make him sad all over again. Mostly, all I can think about right now is Carrie and the way she's pressing her nose up against the window while she rides in my lap, just like a dog. So I tell Serena, "Not really. Nothing that can't wait 'til we're, you know . . ."

"Alone?" Serena finishes for me.

I nod, though of course she can't see me. "How about you?"

"I thought you'd never ask," she says. Then she unloads about how Mazen has decided, since the weather is warmer, he's going to run at night. How this burns her up because, until recently, they've been running together after lunch before he goes back to the office. "He doesn't even ask me if I want to run with him now. He just comes home for dinner, all hot and sweaty, and says what a great run he's had. And is the lasagna ready." I know Serena is shaking her head in this way she has, like she's shaking water out of her hair. "I mean, it's like he's lost his sensitive side and doesn't even know it's missing!"

"Ouch!" I tell her. "That smarts!" I'm imagining Maze and his red Nikes jogging in the park near their house while Serena's stuck at home fixing pasta.

"You got that straight." There's a pause while she lets herself go there. "He says I've got enough to do with my gallery show coming up. That I'm burning calories just by hanging canvas."

Serena is a terrific painter, and I ought to know. I still love the smell of turpentine from growing up with all those half-finished canvases perched like bright birds all over the house. "The show's in a few weeks, right?" I ask.

"Yeah, let's see what new excuse he cooks up then." Serena sighs like the drama queen we both know she is. "'Til then? If I want to stay fit, I guess I'll have to do it on my own."

That's when I remember *New Body, New Self.* And *S-E-X.* Talk about feeling alone! There's three of us in this truck, but Carrie is only a kitten, and my father? He gets a free pass just by being male. He'll never have to worry that any minute he's going to start bleeding and have to walk around with a tampon inside him. Plus he doesn't have to look forward to celebrating this revolting development like it's some kind of birthday party. "As soon as you graduate from kid to teenager," Daddy is always promising, "we'll be off the road and in our own brand-new house."

So my dreaded first "monthly" will bring with it not only what my book refers to as "womanhood's wake-up call," but it will also put me one step closer to a *real* school that stays in one place. And a *real* home that doesn't move all over the map. Both of which would be (A) totally boring, (B) like prison, and (C) the end of everything I love, everything I need like breathing.

Naturally, with Daddy sitting across from me, I can't complain about all this to Serena. No offense, but this is definitely girl talk. I decide to wait until I see her in person. We should pick up our last load in Springfield and be in Chapel Hill three days from now. So when Serena finishes her Mazen Blues, I don't try to have a girls-only discussion in front of my father. Instead, I start a conversation he absolutely *needs* to overhear. "Hmmm," I say, my voice lowered as if I don't want him to eavesdrop. "There *is* something you and I really, really need to talk about." I can feel Daddy getting interested, even though his profile looks all serious and Road Warrior-like.

"What's cooking?" Serena asks. She's interested, too.

"Well," I stage-whisper, drawing things out, making sure I've got my father's full attention. "It's about a haircut."

After I say goodbye to Serena, I'm sure that Carrie and Daddy and a new audio mystery will keep me busy. After all, we're less than 1,500 miles from Chapel Hill. And we'll be devouring turkey legs and funnel cakes in Memphis, our halfway stop. Plus, The Peabody hotel, home of the famous marching ducks, is something we never, ever miss. With all that happening down the road, I figure I'm not going to explode with anxiety about getting my period. But it turns out it's impossible to stop thinking about "nature's promise to all women" and my "blossoming body."

It's like waiting for an accident—not one that *might* happen, but one that definitely *will*. It's just a question of when and where. So now, when I eat one too many barbecue nachos and my stomach feels swollen and pitchy, I have to figure out whether I've got indigestion or cramps. ("Nature's reminder that you're old enough to have a baby.") When the indigestion doesn't quit, should I ask Daddy to stop at the drugstore? ("Super?" "Regular?" "Slender?" How do *I* know? I'm only eleven, for crying out loud!) Will it hurt? Will it be messy? Will it happen today? Tomorrow? Next month? Next year?

New Body, New Self says I should "ask a female relative, maybe your mother, about menses." (Why isn't it called "womenses," anyway?) After lunch, I decide that's just what I'll do. Of course, when your nearest female relative is in a green marble box on the dashboard, more wish and memory than flesh and blood, girl-talk gets a little complicated. So once he's full of his favorite deep-fried mozzarella, I ask Daddy to please walk Carrie on the rope leash I've rigged up for her. It's tied to one of his old socks, which works perfectly as a halter for tiny Carrie the Escape Cat. "I saw a neat fitness park behind the restaurant," I tell him. "Carrie could chew clover and throw up while you do the rope climb."

I feel almost guilty at how easy this is. "Don't you want to come?" My father is already shrugging into his sweatshirt, our newest team member rubbing against his legs.

"Actually? I have some reading to do." I hold up the new book, wave those lady shapes around. Daddy nods, tells me right away,

"Good for you, Haz." Then, Carrie tucked under one arm, he stops halfway out of the cab. "Lock up as soon as I leave, okay?"

After they're out of sight, I lean into the dashboard and look long and hard at the green box. I get the same warm feeling I always do, like wind in summer, only softer. I open the glove compartment, and I know just which photo I want. I scrounge through the pile in there 'til I find the old Polaroid from before I was born. The one where Mom's wearing that blouse embroidered with roses, the one where I can look straight in her eyes.

I look right at the picture, even though it's all bent and cracked from my holding it so much. "Can I share something," I ask my mother, "woman to woman?" I tell her how scary this whole "journey to adulthood" feels. After all, if my father means what he says about quitting trucking so I can attend a high school with peers who will encourage "my full potential"—which, if you ask me, is almost as scary as "my blossoming body," I'm on a fast track to a frilly canopy bed, to school bells telling me where to go and what to do. I add that it feels really awkward to have nobody but my father to talk about S-E-X with. And that I'd like to get it all out of my head, but that it's like when you try *not* to think about an earworm, the song just keeps repeating over and over and . . . well, you know.

I tell that old photo everything—and then I just sit, same as always, with Mom's picture in my lap and my eyes closed. I let the feeling of her halo hair, her smile fall around me. And I wait. Pretty soon, I hear a sound, like someone laughing behind a closed door. It's so real and so close, I straighten up and open my eyes. I find I'm looking straight through the front window at the white face of the moon. It's just above the dash, riding in the afternoon sky, waiting to rise. There are wispy, rose-colored clouds all around it. And yes, it's looking right *back* at me, but this time I see something I've never noticed before. That's not a man in the moon; it's a *woman*. And she's heard every single word.

SONGS FOR THE ROAD

Carrie makes me smile all the time. If I'm reading one of Willa's movie zines, she crawls between me and the page I'm looking at. If I'm listening to an old Surf's Up song in my ear pods, she claws at my sleeve and whines 'til I stop. And it's not because she's sad, like I am, that my favorite group broke up. It's because her furry brain has hatched another Carrie Original and she can't wait to try it out on me. As soon as I stop what I'm doing and look at her, she starts singing. I mean it, Willa's singing dog has nothing on my cat—and I didn't even train Carrie; she's a natural.

She holds her head so far back, it's as if she's staring at something on the ceiling. Only, her eyes are shut, and she sways like someone in a trance. Then she starts yowling in little bursts, singing in a sort of Morse code. *RAUEEEE. Ra. AHHH-EEE. Ra. Ra.*

Oh, I know it's not real Morse code because Daddy and I studied that in our unit on the Second World War. (Part of the test was for me to spell my whole name in dots and dashes.) But if you lean in close to Carrie and listen hard, you can hear a kind of message, a pattern, another language. *Ra-waaaah. WAAAHUEEEE. EEEE-ah. Ra-eeee.*

Tonight, though, I figure our new team member is too tired for vocal gymnastics. We were late out of Denver, so we're spending the night in Kansas instead of Missouri. Daddy tried to make up some of the time by driving extra far after dinner. When we're ready for our bedtime ritual with those Day-Glo stars on the roof, Carrie leads the way. She races up her sheet ladder and settles in under the blanket. It's like my first nights on the road, only instead of the stuffed teddy Serena sent me off with when I was four, I'm curled up with my new kitten. "Good night, Big Bear," I whisper to Daddy over Carrie's dark head. I reach up to trace the Big Dipper with one sleepy finger.

"Good night, Little Bear," he tells me. He taps the Little Dipper's handle, then kisses my forehead. He draws the curtain across my bunk and turns on the reading light above his own. He's been plowing through the same book for three nights now. It was written by a guy he used to teach with in North Carolina. I don't think he likes it very much, though, because when I ask him if it's any good, he waves the novel in the air and tells me, "Let's just say you've got no competition here, Haz. This is *not* the Great American Novel." Then he sighs like he's doing homework and opens the book again.

I drift off with Carrie who, it turns out, is not as tired as I thought. In fact, it feels like only a minute after I hear Daddy turn his second page that my bunkmate comes up with a brand-new chartbuster.

She sits straight up under the blanket like a tiny ghost, and then? She lets loose! The short and long howls come really fast, and that ghost is wriggling so much, I know it's going to be out of its blanket any second.

Mwaaaaa-ee-MWAAA-ha-HAAAAAAA.

"Shhhhhh!" I say. Then I reach under the sheet and pull her out. "You're going to bother Daddy," I tell her.

Mwwaaa-ha-ha-EEEOUWWWW-ha-Yeeeee, Carrie replies.

"Haz?" Daddy calls up to me. "You okay?"

"Sure, no problem." When I hear another page turn, I put my hand over Chatterbox Carrie's mouth. "You want to hear a story?" I ask her. She doesn't answer, partly because it's hard to send Morse code through someone's hand, and partly because, well, she's too fascinated by my glow-in-the-dark stars.

"Don't worry, they're not real bears," I assure her. "That's just how stars look if you're trying to make pictures out of them. That way, tomorrow night you can remember right where you left them."

Carrie turns her head to stare at all the stars at once. I move my hand away from her mouth, and instead of singing her latest hit again, she takes her big green eyes off the stars and looks at me. It's as if she's saying, *Well? Where's the story?*

"I don't have a book with pictures," I tell her. "So we'll have to use the stars, okay?" My kitten puts a paw on my fingers, then lays her head on my chest as if she's trying to hear my heart. "Once there was a mama bear and a baby bear," I begin. "And the mama bear loved her little girl bear very, very much."

I don't know if Carrie remembers her cat mama, her people, or if she even understands a single word I'm saying. I don't know why Denver's mom threw her out like garbage, or why she changed her mind. "They did everything together, those bears, because the daughter bear loved to copy her mother."

No dots and dashes. Carrie is quiet, but those big eyes of hers are still open, still watching. Which I figure translates to "So?"

"So, one day when it got very cold, mama bear told her baby it was time to hibernate." I check in with Carrie. "That means it was time to go to sleep in a deep, dark cave," I explain.

When you've held a real live baby in your arms and her eyes looked into yours until she fell alseep? You think about her. A *lot*. And you want her never to be unhappy. Never to wonder where her mom is.

"Baby bear looked around the cave. 'Can I hibernate, too?' she asked.

"'Of course, you can,' her mama told her. 'And when we wake up, we'll have some Klondike bars!'

"'With nuts?' asked baby bear."

There's a sniffling mini-snort from the bunk underneath us.

"Daddy?" I push myself up on one elbow and call down to the bottom bunk. "I know you're listening."

"Am not," he says.

"Are too. You haven't turned a single page in your book."

"How do you know?"

"I can hear when you do."

"From all the way up there? Cannot."

"Can too."

Even though I can't see him, I know my father's shaking his head. "Sleep tight, Little Bear." He turns out his light, and I hear the whoosh and then the snap as he closes his own curtains.

Carrie's eyes are finally closed. I yawn, turn over to face the wall, and get ready to dream more of the story. "G'night, Big Bear."

A PROMISE

Finally we pull into the warehouse outside Springfield. It's tiny as warehouses go, with only four bays, so it doesn't take long to pick up our new load of—wait for it—*cowboy boots*! When he showed us the load sheet, Mazen made some scary-bad jokes about how my father could stop homeschooling me and send me to "boot camp" instead. Or about how cowboys die with their boots on because they don't want to stub their toes when they kick the bucket. Daddy and I groaned, but honestly? From the pictures on the boxes, these boots were made for showing off more than working or riding the range. They come in all colors and are made of skins from cows, alligators, snakes, and even ostriches. They're embroidered with cacti and flowers and eagles and bucking broncos.

All those fancy boots are stacked in pallets, and it takes no time to arrange them in four rows and strap them into the truck. We're on our way to Memphis in less than an hour, headed for a city both Daddy and I love to visit. And who wouldn't? We've been to Elvis Presley's home, Graceland, about thirty kazillion times, and we never pass up the chance to overeat on Beale Street or to watch those celebrity ducks parade through the lobby of The Peabody.

Long before I was born, even before Daddy was born, somebody thought it would be funny to let ducks swim in the famous hotel's fountain. It was! It still is! Every day now a tiny family of ducks rides an elevator down from the roof of the hotel and then waddles right into the lobby. And every day hundreds of tourists come to watch them.

It's a good thing we're leaving Missouri early, because we've got nearly three hundred miles of road between here and the 5 p.m. duck march. I decide to do my homework on the way so we'll have plenty of time to fit everything in. After we stop to grab breakfast, I walk the cat, set up the GPS, and then? I hit the books.

Or *book*, singular, in this case. I've nearly finished *New Body, New Self.* And you know what? It turns out this unit on human reproduction, or what *New Body* calls "the miracle of life," isn't half as scary as I thought it would be. It isn't even gross. It's pretty much the same as what I watched a pair of dogs do in a parking lot behind a KFC in Cincinnati when I was eight. Ditto, a library documentary I saw last year about dolphins mating. (They nose-kiss a lot!) Sure, it's more complicated with humans, but that's because boys probably want to get to know you before they try to make babies with you. And girls may want to grow up and drive a truck or write a movie first. Besides, no one can make babies unless the time is right, and that's where your "monthly" comes in.

This is the part I wasn't sure about, but now I get it. Only, Daddy can't give me a unit test yet because they left the teacher's guide out of this home-study pack. "Would you believe it?" My father couldn't stop snort-laughing when he turned the mailer upside down and nothing came out. "Guess I'll have to wait 'til you're done, Haz," he told me. "Maybe then you can teach me a thing or two, okay?"

Of course he was kidding. I know Daddy knows about this stuff, and I also know that last year, he and a redheaded night clerk at the Econo Lodge in Houston spent the night in her apartment. He tried to be quiet as a mouse when he came back to our room at 5 a.m., but unless it was a mouse trapped in a bag of marbles, he didn't exactly succeed. When I asked him where he'd been, he looked kind of sad and very, very tired. "Learning the hard way" was all he said. We left before checkout time, so I guess that even though that woman's hair probably reminded him of Mom's, their time together wasn't what *New Body, New Self* calls "a celebration of deep trust and love."

Now, even though I've just read the last page of the book, I don't tell Daddy. I want to spend the rest of the drive working on my pitch for the movie. So I turn back to the middle, take out my new journal, and get to work. I'm just describing how we put Carrie in charge of watching the truck while we shop or eat or pee when I look up to find Daddy watching me write. He tries to check out the journal page closest to him, but luckily he loves cursive and that's how he taught me to write. Which means he can't really read my loopy script and drive at the same time. "Wow!" is all he says. "You're taking notes! I'm impressed." He squints at my long-tailed consonants and squirrelly vowels, then gives up and turns back to the road.

I write straight through 'til it's time to eat, which means I break my own personal record for fewest bathroom breaks ever. I decide that it might be a good idea to give a singing cat a supporting role in *Wheels of Fire*. Especially one that sings in Morse code.

After we pick up lunch, I take my tuna sandwich, my book, and my journal to the bottom bunk in back. That way, Daddy can't read what I'm writing, and I can put my leftovers on the floor for Carrie. (Tuna is her second-favorite, after bacon cheeseburgers.)

"Is there anything you want to ask me?" Daddy's voice is loud enough to reach me in back, but he says the words so fast, I'm pretty sure he hopes there isn't. I just smile and say no, then bury my nose again in *New Body, New Self*. Once Leonardo is doing sixty-five miles per hour, I go back to writing my pitch. *Truck dogs guard their rigs by barking and looking fierce,* I write.

"You sure you don't have any questions on all this?" Daddy's looking at me in the rearview.

"Positive." I don't even glance up. I crouch so low over the book, my hair is brushing the tails of my *g*'s and *y*'s: *Our truck cat sings in code. It is probably a secret message to mice. Because we don't have* any!

"Listen, I'm here if you do—"

"Nope."

I guess my father is pretty surprised. I mean, I almost *always* have questions. Even about long division and tectonics. About the Industrial Revolution and bar graphs. Maybe he thinks he's not doing his homeschooling best?

"Daddy?" Now I look straight at his eyes in the mirror. They're all hopeful and ready to impart wisdom. "Does The Peabody allow cats?"

He sounds very surprised, but he figures out what I mean. "As in, will we be able to take Carrie to see the ducks walk in the lobby?"

"On a leash, of course." I can't wait to show our kitty those famous ducks strutting through the hotel.

"Oh, those ducks don't need a leash, Hazmat. They know their way from the elevator to the fountain."

"Da-ad!" He thinks he's being funny, but he's bordering on annoying. "You know what I mean!"

"Sure I do." His eyes aren't smiling anymore or intent on imparting knowledge. They're all serious and let's-be-adults-about-this. "But I'm afraid Memphis's fanciest hotel and my animal-loving daughter aren't likely to agree on how to deal with pets."

He's looking back at me in the mirror again, so I guess he sees how upset I am. "Hey," he tells me. "We'll fix Carrie up with some kitty treats and that plastic bottle you glued ears on." He winks. "She'll be just fine in the truck for a few hours."

"But you know how she loves to people-watch." I picture my kitten all alone with the dumb mouse I made out of an old soda bottle filled with dried peas. I picture her waiting for us to come back, batting that noisy toy around and wondering why it's taking us so long to pick up burgers. "It's not like we'd be spending the night or anything," I say. "Besides, anyplace that allows ducks should allow cats, right?"

I feel tears start up just before Daddy takes the cell from the dash. He passes it over the front seat. "Check with Mr. Google," he says. "You have a point."

My father and I have a rule: Our cell phone is strictly for calls, maps, and research; we don't use it for games or texting or putting mustaches on selfies and sending them out into the world. Which is why, even though I wish I could sneak a quick peek at Willa's JimJam account, I know better. (Besides, every time I do, nothing's changed. All I see are those same old moves of hers, the ones she showed me before she slipped away in that pickup.)

What if I'm right? What if Carrie can come with us for once? I mean, we're always leaving her in the truck. Why shouldn't she be in on some of the fun we have? I switch to the phone's browser as Daddy drives onto the breakdown lane. I click the little microphone icon and ask the Internet: "Can pets watch the Peabody ducks?" It takes me less than a minute to find the hotel's pet policies spelled out on their website. It turns out I'm more right than wrong—but not quite right enough: for a fee, The Peabody will house your pet, up to seventy-five pounds. But watching the ducks? "Animal guests are strictly prohibited during our twice daily duck marches."

I read the policy out loud to Daddy, then I tell our kitten, "Sorry, Carrie. No cats allowed." Before I can lean down to give her a consolation pat, she jumps up and sits right on top of *New Body, New Self.* "But we've got two hours to Memphis," I add, scratching behind her ears. "And I promise I'll put a tail on your bottle mouse, okay?"

When Daddy's got Leonardo up to speed again, I stop scratching those soft black cat ears and start whispering into them instead. "I promise something else, too," I tell the most adorable cat in the entire solar system, including all eight planets and their moons and any future dwarves like Jupiter we might end up discovering: "I don't care what that dumb hotel's rules are, you are *not* going to miss that duck parade!"

SITTING DUCKS

It takes two more hours of driving to reach Memphis. In most other cities, we'd spend another half hour trying to find parking. (When you're looking for a lot that will take a forty-foot trailer, there aren't a ton of places that put out the welcome mat. And the apps that promise to find them? Well, let's just say they break that promise a lot.) But Daddy and I have been coming to Memphis for so many years, we've made friends with the manager of a motel that's right downtown. He lets us park in the back lot for half the overnight room rate. (Trust me, that's a deal.)

As we leave Leonardo and Carrie on Second Street and walk in the direction of The Peabody, I tell Daddy I've forgotten my Elvis sweatshirt—how can we visit Memphis without it? He hands me the key and I run back to the truck; after I've jogged back to him and we're on our way for real, he does more of his by-now-famous headshaking. "Seventy-five degrees doesn't feel much like sweatshirt weather, Haz," he says.

"I don't want to lose this sweatshirt again," I explain. Neither of us wants to go through what we did last year, when I left my brand-new Graceland souvenir in a rest stop outside Atlanta, then spent an extra two hours driving back to find it.

My father sighs, resigned to going downtown with a cold-blooded wacko in a hoodie, then tries to grab my hand. But I need that hand—both hands, in fact—to hold something else right now. It turns out the front pocket of my sweatshirt is pretty heavy and *very wiggly*. I just wish my stowaway didn't have such sharp claws.

"We're off!" I charge ahead of my father down the sidewalk. "Hurry up, Daddy. I don't want to be late."

I pass a ton of pedestrians, most of them headed in the same direction we are. By the time I walk into The Peabody, a huge crowd has already gathered around the central fountain in the lobby. They're lined up along the route the ducks will take back to their penthouse on the roof. Everyone is snapping away, cell phones and cameras flashing and clicking up a mini electrical storm.

In the middle of all the excitement, four female mallards with brown feathers and bright eyes and one male with a satiny green head are paddling calmly, circling around and around the fountain in a marble pond. By the time Daddy catches up to me, he's winded but happy. He grins and puts his arm around my shoulder. He loves being back here, taking part in what he calls our Thirteenth Running of the Ducks.

Me? Daddy's arm feels heavier than it should, and my sweatshirt is making me really, really hot. But the people around us are all laughing and talking, so I'm the only one who notices that, not only is my sweatshirt heating up fast, it's also . . . singing! *Eee-mwameee-mwa-mwaeeeowwww!* Uh-oh. A few feet from us in the crowd, a little boy with a mohawk, a Peabody Ducks tee, and excellent hearing points at me.

"Hey!" he says, tugging on his mother's purse strap. "There's something in there!"

He's pointing directly at my sweatshirt. Fortunately, his mom is so busy taking pictures, she doesn't pay any attention. The boy lets go of his mother and comes toward me just in time to hear the second chorus of Carrie's latest and greatest: *Mwaaa-ee-mwaa-eow-ee.*

"Hey!" Without taking his eyes off me and my singing belly, the boy tries to snap his mother out of her photo frenzy. "Hey, you gotta hear this!"

Eee-mwaa-eow-ee-yowww-mwa. My sweatshirt and I turn and walk to the other side of my father. There's another kid on this side, a girl much closer to my age than Mohawk Boy. This will undoubtedly trigger Daddy's "Let's make a new friend for Hazel" mania. But anything is worth keeping my stowaway under wraps.

"Do you love this show as much as we do?" Yep. That's Daddy, talking to the girl, who's not even looking at us, and to her mom, who is looking.

The mother answers for them both. "We come once a month, right, Jess?" Her daughter decides she'd rather look at me than either of the adults in our neighborhood. She shrugs her shoulders, rolls her eyes.

Without knowing it, Jess's mom has given my father the opening he needs. He's on it like peanut butter on bread: "Jess, this is my daughter, Hazel," he says, beaming at us both. "Hazel, meet Jess."

Silence, except for the crowd noises around us (and my stomach, which continues to growl, literally).

"Jess?" The girl's mother smiles at Daddy, tries again. "What do you say?"

More silence until, finally, Jess takes a wild guess at the answer. "Hello?" she says.

Mercifully, a whole new storm of furious camera clicks starts up behind us, then loud, recorded march music pours out of the speakers hanging overhead. Jess and I both turn, with everyone else in the lobby, to watch the tall man who's just gotten off the elevator in the hallway behind us.

The Duckmaster, dressed in a fancy red uniform with gold trim, strides out of the elevator and marches straight up to the fountain. He's carrying a cane topped by a silver duck-head handle. He's waving it to the music and sweating even more than I am. When he stops and holds up his cane, the hotel's five feathered celebrities swim to the front of the fountain. The Duckmaster places three duck-sized steps beside the fountain and unrolls a length of crimson carpet that leads back through the crowd toward the elevators. Then he taps the top step with his cane and the ducks assemble there, shake their feathers, and step, one at a time, onto the carpet and down into the crowd.

I've watched these ducks parade to and from that fountain over a dozen times now. But it's still sillier and more fun than just about anything. I crouch down like I'm trying to get a good view and I unzip my sweatshirt pocket, just enough to make sure there's a view from in there—of the steps, the pond, and, of course, the five waddling stars of the show. The music is still blaring, and down here at floor level, I'm pretty sure no one else can hear how much louder the singing inside my sweatshirt has gotten. Carrie must really love the show!

I do, too. It's so much fun to watch the way those celebrity ducks take their time along the "parade route" to the elevators. They get distracted by everything, and people are encouraging them to stop and pose. Kids call them ("Here, duckie! Here, duckie!"); grown-ups make imitation duck sounds and hold out their hands; and even though feeding the ducks is definitely not allowed, I see cookies and bread slices being waved in the air.

I guess after a full day on display in the lobby, the mallards don't want to give up all the attention. They're moseying along as if they can't hear that brisk music at all, pausing to inspect a toddler's outstretched fingers, peering like starlets into the cameras, and checking out intriguing crumbs on the carpet.

The trouble is that someone else has been checking *them* out too. I probably left my sweatshirt pocket too far open because all of a sudden? It's empty!

The ducks are only a few yards down the red plush when they come to a full stop. Like a group of choreographed dancers, they spin in a single frightened clump, then charge off in the opposite direction, back toward the fountain.

An intense and very speedy black fur ball races after them. It pursues them down the carpet as squawks and screams overwhelm the canned Sousa march music.

"Carrie!" I don't care who hears me now; I'm screaming. I stumble up, nearly knocking down Jess and her mother and hurrying toward my runaway kitten. But she's got too big a lead on me. She's chasing all five of those famous ducks, and she's closing in *fast*.

The Duckmaster is totally flustered; he's stopped marching and started yelling. "Hey! Come back here!" He's waving his cane, but not in a snappy, musical way. "Who brought that animal in here?"

Behind the Duckmaster, Daddy has joined the backward parade to the fountain. He doesn't look any happier than I feel. And he seems to be a whole lot madder. But Carrie is having the time of her kitten life. She's pretty proud of herself now that she's cornered the ducks by the pond, which they can't waddle back to since the red steps on which they reached it have been pulled away. My cat draws back onto her small haunches, then mock pounces toward each duck in turn.

The mallards honk in alarm and ruffle their feathers just enough to keep her repeating her threatening pantomime.

Spectators, meanwhile, are in alarm mode, scurrying uselessly, first after the ducks, then after their tiny tormentor. Finally, once the lone male duck figures out how to fly, rather than march, into the fountain, the four hens take to the air too. Not all of them head for the fountain, though, one choosing to settle in the large chandelier directly above it, another landing on the balcony that runs around the lobby one floor up. The guests who have come out of their rooms to watch the proceedings from above begin to scurry either to or away from the airborne ducks, and the pandemonium spreads. By now there's splashing and slipping below, laughter and yelling at balcony level, and lots of squawking everywhere.

Mohawk Boy is pointing at us again. And laughing. "I told you! I told you!" But again, his mother isn't listening. Instead, she's shaking water out of one of her high heels. Jess and her mother have disappeared, probably because, well, who wants to be trampled by stampeding people or doused by flying ducks?

Down at ground level, I spot Carrie trying to scale the sheer stone wall of the fountain. Fancy Italian marble and kitten claws don't mix, so she's slipping back down over and over. Willpower gets her up almost a body length before she slides back down again, only to repeat her banana-peel move. I can't fight my way to her through the crowd, but my father, who has pushed past the Duckmaster, is already there. He sloshes through the water around the pond, scoops Carrie up, pins her to his side, and carries her back to me.

He doesn't give me the Voldemort scowl. He doesn't scold or yell. He just hands me my kitten, and then? I burst into tears. No one else seems to notice that we've arrested the perp; they're all too busy chasing ducks, grabbing photo ops, or screaming. All I can think about is getting Carrie to the truck. I put Carrie back in my sweatshirt, dodge in and out of the crowd, and, finally, find a door that leads to the street. We're outside on the sidewalk before Daddy catches up to us. He says very quietly, "We've got to go back, you know."

I'm holding my kitten and crying at the same time. When I realize we can't make a clean getaway, I start crying even harder. I guess he's afraid I'll drop Carrie, because now Daddy lifts her, legs dangling, out of my arms, before he adds, "And Hazel? You've got a LOT of explaining to do!"

SORRY IS A HARD PLACE TO BE

Daddy has told me three times now that I will have to apologize "in no uncertain terms." I'm not sure what that means, but I'm guessing it won't be fun. The only reason we don't turn right around and head back to the hotel is Carrie. "This orphan kitty," my father insists, "is not the guilty party. Besides," he adds, not smiling even a little bit, "I don't think bringing Carrie back to the scene of the crime will help our cause."

So we take Carrie back to the rig and I set her up in her blanket on my bunk. We leave her water bowl on the floor, pull the kitty litter tray out from under the bed, and tell her to "watch the fort." But sadly, we do *not* head to Beale Street for dinner or for beignets and music downtown. Instead, we head back to The Peabody, where I've got a date with the Duckmaster.

But before that, we do what we couldn't do a few minutes ago, on account of my waterworks—we talk. Or Daddy does, anyway. "Why, kiddo?" His voice is soft. Let down. Fed up. "Why'd you pull this caper? It's not like Carrie hasn't guarded the truck before."

I can't look at him. I focus, instead, on the window fronts we pass. All the stores are getting ready for Easter, so there are bunnies and fluffy chicks everywhere. Bunnies and chicks and mountains of chocolate. "We've left her alone every time we go for meals," my father tells me. "In fact, I think she kind of likes being a guard cat."

We're walking side by side now, but I'm too ashamed to take his hand. "Hey," he adds, sounding a bit more like himself. "That cat can take care of herself. The way I see it, she'll be old enough to help us *drive* pretty soon."

I know this silly joke is sort of like holding hands. It's supposed to make me smile, but it backfires. I picture Carrie turned into a giant, grown-up cat and I start crying all over again. Harder and harder 'til I can't see anything but tears. I stop walking.

"What? What's wrong?" Daddy stops beside me, and the late sun throws his shadow around me, cuts me off from the bunnies and chocolate.

I stand there and let the sobbing and trembling take me over. When they finally die down, I tell him, "I—I don't *want* our cat to grow up." I feel the tears drawing an old-fashioned mustache down each side of my mouth, but I don't even try to brush them away. "I want her to stay little."

Daddy doesn't say anything. He just opens his arms, right there in the middle of the busy sidewalk. And even though I'm a preteen and in a little over a year I'll be an actual teenager like Willa, I step into that hug of his.

"I don't want my cat to get big and re—responsible." I choke on the word, holding on tight now and sobbing again. "I don't want her to go away and have babies and—and get too old to have fun."

"Judging from that romp with the ducks?" Daddy tells my right ear. "I think we've got a long wait 'til Crazy Carrie figures out what responsibility is. Besides . . ." He steps back, lifts my chin, and looks into my soupy eyes. "I spent years running away from a responsibility that turned out to be one of the biggest joys of my life."

"Me?" I ask, knowing the answer.

"These last seven years, watching you grow? They've given me more pleasure than I can ever say. And you know what else?"

It's okay to stand away from a hug that you know you can come back to anytime you want. I sniff, try out a beginner smile. "What?" I ask.

My father brushes my hair away from my eyes. I smell Carrie and sun and soap on his hands. "Growing up doesn't mean you have to stop having fun."

I'm full-on smiling now. "Promise?" I ask.

Daddy pulls away, both hands on my shoulders. "No guarantees," he says. "But there are plenty of adults who know how to have a good time. I hope you're looking at one," he says. "And in case you've forgotten, we're on our way to see another two in Chapel Hill."

"We are?" I wipe under one eye. "I thought we were going to pay for the mess I just made." My stomach remembers I have to apologize, and I almost wish we'd hit traffic on 70 and never made the Thirteenth Running of the Ducks.

"Oh, we'll pay," Daddy agrees. "But I'm betting that a man who dresses up in a red soldier suit and leads a duck parade—I mean, how tough can it be to make him see the funny side of all this?"

I feel better. "You mean the duck in the chandelier? That *was* kind of incredible."

"Sure." My father takes my arm, steers us again toward the hotel. "And what about that woman on the balcony? Did you hear her yelling, 'There's a duck in my bed!'?"

I think about what we've just been through. "The thing is," I say, "how long can the funny side of all that last?"

"What do you mean?"

"Well, after we left, someone had to calm down the guests."

Daddy nods. "And round up the ducks."

I fall behind, toting up the damage. "And wipe down the floor. And clean up the fountain."

"So, what do you think?" he asks. "Maybe this calls for clown suits?"

"Dad!" I tell him. "We can't treat this like a joke." Everything can't be funny all the time, right? "We have to go in there and apologize."

"We?" It's Daddy's turn to stop in his tracks. "*We?*"

I stop, too, and the whole crazy afternoon plays itself over in my head. No, *we* didn't smuggle Carrie into the hotel. *We* didn't open our pocket so she could get a pond-side view of the ducks.

And *we* didn't kind of forget to tell anyone what we had up our sleeve—er, sweatshirt.

"Daddy? Will you come with me?"

He takes my hand. We walk like that all the way back to the hotel.

We don't need clown costumes after all. The Duckmaster is really nice; his name is Francis Sheldon, and now that he's out of uniform and sitting in his messy office in front of a big fan, he looks a little shorter and a *lot* cooler. He pulls up two chairs, pushing papers and cups off them so we can sit down. Then he listens to my apology. It includes the facts that I'm only eleven and that this is the first time I've smuggled a cat. I also offer to use the allowance I've saved to pay for the cleanup. When I'm finished, he shakes his head. "Actually," he says, "a lot of what happened this afternoon was my fault. I've kept these ducks too long."

"Too long?" My father doesn't know it, but he always telegraphs a punch line before he says it. He squints, and then he folds his arms like he's daring you not to laugh. "Are they asking for a raise?"

Mr. Sheldon thinks Daddy's joke is a lot funnier than I do. They both laugh, and then the Duckmaster is shaking his head again. "No," he says. "It's just that the farm that sends them to us clips their wings to keep them from flying away. But their feathers grow back, and they start to get tame in just a few months. That's why those ducks were cozying up to the crowd today. And why one of them made it to the balcony."

"You mean," I ask, "you forgot to give your ducks a haircut?"

"Not quite." Mr. Sheldon laughs by himself this time. (Daddy apparently still doesn't think haircuts are very funny.) "What I *did* forget, though, is to trade them in for a whole new team."

"Where does the old team go?"

"Oh, we send them back to the farm." When he smiles, the Duckmaster gets tiny creases beside his eyes just like Daddy does.

"Wait!" I think about all the parades I've been to here. "Does that mean we've never seen the same ducks twice?"

Those smile creases get deeper. "Probably not," Mr. Sheldon tells us. "Hopefully by this time next week the ducks you saw today will have hung up their stars and be leading regular, ordinary duck lives again."

"Like having babies and stuff?" Thanks, *New Body, New Self.* Did I really need to ask that?

"Sure," Mr. Sheldon says. "Once they're home again, they can mate, have ducklings, and best of all, they can forget everything I've taught them." He grins. "In fact, if they want, when their wings are grown all the way back, they can fly off for good." He glances toward the empty fountain. "Why, in another few years, those birds will probably have traveled more miles than most of us ever will."

Daddy and I look at each other and smile. We don't say it, of course, but we know a thing or two about traveling. We say goodbye and shake hands with the Duckmaster again. He invites us to come back anytime. He says the red carpet is always out. Just not for a certain cat who shall remain nameless.

"I guess it's for the best," Daddy tells me on the walk back to the truck. "Those ducks need the chance to have babies, swim in a real pond, and migrate, just like other birds."

I remember Carmen's song about birds with clipped wings, about how they fly away. "Migrate?" I ask.

"Yep. Mallards are great flyers, and they move with the sun. They hit the road at the first sign of frost."

"Like us?"

Daddy just smiles, but I'm on a roll. "So I'm all for migrating and swimming," I tell him. "But could we skip the having-babies part?"

Now Daddy's laughing so hard, he has to stop walking. "Guess your homework has given you lots to think about, huh?"

It sure has! Which is why, once we spot Leonardo and a certain small face looking for us out the window, I make a silent promise to myself: nobody's going to clip *my* wings—not with a full tank of gas for tomorrow's haul and the world's most talented feline waiting to sing us to sleep.

We're scheduled to drop off the cowboy boots at a giant Western Wear store outside Winston-Salem and get into Chapel Hill about three o'clock, just in time for sweet tea and honeysuckle biscuits on Serena's porch. But first, we have to wait while the store's automated warehouse system unloads and stacks our pallets. Daddy's inside getting some paperwork signed while I watch through the tiny window in the waiting room as a team of busy mechanical robots runs between our truck and the warehouse shelves. The bots look like giant bees storing honey, their treadmill bottoms moving back and forth as a small crane on top empties and stacks, empties and stacks. Empties . . . and then an AGV (Automated Guided Vehicle) pushes too hard or loses its grip or who knows what, and a bunch of pallets go flying off a top shelf.

It's like dominoes falling. The whole row of tall metal shelves collapses, and one after another, pallets and boxes fall to the floor, raining on top of each other, scattering tissue paper and cowboy boots everywhere. Pointy alligator-skin toes, snakeskin, and calfskin heels poke out of the mess of paper and leather and cardboard tops and bottoms. Because machines don't know when to stop, one bot follows the first, and pretty soon there are three of them dumping their pallets into thin air, where the fallen shelf used to be. By the dozens, then by the hundreds, there are boots, boots everywhere.

"Hey." Daddy comes to sit beside me, clipboard in hand. But I'm out of my chair, my face pressed against the tiny oval window in the warehouse door.

I crook my pointer finger at him like I've got a pretty big secret brewing, and then I back away from the window so he can see. In about two seconds, he's laughing out loud.

I can hardly keep the happy-smug out of my voice. "So," I ask, "is this the shiny, high-tech future that's going to make you and me obso—obso . . . ?"

"Obsolete." My father straightens out the tongue twister for me, then gets a phone book so I don't have to stand on tiptoe to see through the window. Side by side, we watch the mess swell like a wave that's now covering the whole warehouse floor. Back and forth go those busy-bee loader bots, their skinny claws clutching and releasing, clutching and releasing.

The piles grow, the boots crumple together, and Daddy and I laugh 'til the tears come. And the relief. Because it isn't just funny, it's also very good news: automated warehouses don't always run smoothly. And if AGVs can't be counted on, how can robo-trucks?

Computers can't read traffic and other drivers; they can't navigate in a snowstorm, change a blown-out tire, or back into a narrow shipping bay. They can't help at the scene of an accident or deliver babies or figure out how to deal with downtown traffic.

So now, as two humanoids from the warehouse crew rush onto the scene and the boot-hurling robots screech high-pitched, grinding noises as they're turned off, I'm pretty sure the future of trucking isn't as bleak as I thought. Maybe there's still time for me to grow up, take the CDL, and have a life on the road.

I remember my demon truck. The way it grinned at me with its Lego mouth, the way it told me to stand clear. *Take that!* I think as all those shoeboxes stop tumbling and the warehouse is suddenly quiet.

Those papers Daddy got signed before it rained cowboy boots? They mean it's the warehouse, not Mazen, who'll be responsible for the damage—and for Operation Cleanup Sizes 9–29! It also means we'll have a good story and no bad news to share when we pull into the driveway of my favorite house in the world.

The absolute, hands-down best thing about this Springfield to Wake Forest run? It ends an hour and a half from Mazen and Serena's sand-colored bungalow in Chapel Hill. Maybe it's because I spent the first four years of my life there, but it's the one place besides our truck that always feels like home. For now, we've left the warehouse, we're back up to speed on the highway, and I'm snug in Leonardo's passenger seat with a lap full of Carrie. While our road cat studies the traffic out the window, I'm remembering what April is like in North Carolina.

Warmer weather means Serena will have moved her easel out to the porch. Better still, it means no bugs yet, peepers at night, and at least twenty different birdcalls in the morning. Serena feeds every mouth (and beak and tongue) she sees, so her garden is what I figure Eden was like when Adam got to name all the creepy-crawlies and flyers. Every flower known to spring is in full bloom. Butterflies, hummingbirds, monarch caterpillars, even the deer everyone else wishes would get lost—they're all there, busy and hungry and crowding each other at Serena's bajillion feeders.

I'm in the middle of a home-sweet-home high when Daddy spoils things. "I'll bet Carrie will love it at Mazen's place," he tells me. He's been chatting away, and I've been only half listening. But now I'm on full alert. I shift Carrie in my arms and turn to face my father. He's smiling, folks. Actually smiling!

"She'd better not like it *too* much," I tell him. "We need her with us." Carrie wriggles, tries to get one paw on the glass where those busy mouse-cars are chasing back and forth.

"Maybe we should consider Carrie in this, too."

I'm not sure what "this" is, and I'm positive I don't want to know. Clearly Daddy has a whole "Carrie's Best Interest" speech ready, and it just spills out while I hold my cat tighter and tighter.

"You saw how she acted at the hotel, right? You saw how much she needs to play and have space to run."

"That was *my* fault," I tell him. "I wanted her to share in everything." I flash back to that mad chase across The Peabody's lobby. "I forgot she's a cat, not a person."

"Exactly my point." Daddy reaches over and scratches Carrie under her chin, and she closes her eyes. "Staying locked up in this truck while we're out doing people things might not be in her best interest. Hey." My father turns to look at my face, which can't be a very happy one right now. "I don't mean to make things hard for *you*. I just want to be sure she has the best home possible." We turn off an exit to start the last leg on 15-501 South. At the stoplight, Daddy's hand moves from Carrie's chin to mine. "And who knows? Our favorite animal lover might draw the line at house cats. So what do you say? Shall we let Carrie and Serena work this out by themselves?"

I nod, but I'm pretty sure that after our snuggly sleepovers and sing-alongs, Carrie won't want to give up life on the road. And just to make sure, I decide to put Operation Keep Carrie into effect the minute we reach Chapel Hill. It's a simple two-part plan: first, I'm going to make sure that Serena doesn't fall in love with our cat; and second, I'm going to make sure that our cat doesn't fall in love with Serena!

What do we do as soon as we've parked in the company lot and walked across the street to Maze's house? We HUG! My father hugs Mazen and slaps him on the back. "God, it's good to see you." He hugs him again, then pulls away to stare at his best friend. "Look at that face," he says. "You're just as ugly as ever, but I love you anyway!" And of course he's doing that squinting thing he does when he's teasing.

"I missed you, too." Mazen is close to movie-star handsome and he knows it. Besides, he's heard all Daddy's jokes and one-liners so many times he could probably play both parts all by himself. He grins and hands my father a tall glass of iced tea. Meantime, Serena and I are doing a sort of dance, jumping up and down like little kids with our arms around each other. I have so many things I've been saving up to talk to her about, I don't know where to start. But then I notice the brand-new painting-in-progress on the easel behind us. It's a mother holding a baby, and even though they're both Black, it reminds me of Denver.

Maybe it's the way the baby is looking at the mother, those Velcro eyes. Or maybe it's how the mother is holding her child, just the way Ivy at the Hasty-Mart taught me to hold Denver, with one hand between her legs so she wouldn't fall. The top and bottom of the canvas are nearly blank, covered in the light-gray wash Serena puts underneath all her paintings. But you can see where she's used charcoal to sketch in the mother's hair and her long, flowing skirt.

"Who *are* they?" I ask.

Serena puts her arm around my waist, and we study the painting together. "You can't tell?" she asks. "I've got to add more detail to the hair, of course. And I guess I should lower the forehead a bit. Yeah, and I should probably—"

"It's *you!*" I break away to get closer to the painting, and then I stand back again to bring the patches of color into focus. "That mother is *you!*"

She grins, quiet but proud. She doesn't say it, but I can practically hear her thinking, *It's about time! I wondered how long it would take you to get it!*

"And the baby?" I ask slowly, calmly, just to make sure.

Serena doesn't pat her tummy, but she might as well. Because now I *do* get it.

"Are you . . . ?" I ask. "I mean, are you really—"

"I'm pregnant, Hazmatazz!" She seems relieved to make the news public. "Not due 'til the fall, but it's for real."

I can't even talk. I keep looking at that Serena mother in the painting and thinking about her baby. How it could be a girl like Denver. How I'd get to hold her and play with her anytime I want. It seems kind of dumb now, but the first thing I say is, "I know how to change diapers."

"That's fantastic, Haz!" Serena seems really glad about this weird factoid I pulled out of the air. "You can give me a refresher course." She picks me up under the arms and whirls me around like a doll. "'Cause I haven't done that in ten years!"

"Should you be doing *this*?" I ask her.

We stop whirling and she looks at me. "Doing what?"

"You know," I say. "Picking me up. Stuff like that." *New Body, New Self* has a lot less information about *being* pregnant than it does about *getting* pregnant. But I've seen rules everywhere for people who are expecting. They're on pill bottles and drink labels, on gym equipment and cleaning products: *If you are pregnant or nursing, consult your physician before taking this medication; Dangerous if swallowed or inhaled, especially by small children or pregnant women; If you are overweight or pregnant, talk to your doctor before doing this exercise.*

Serena laughs, but she stops spinning us. "You are as bad as my husband," she tells me, her hands on my shoulders to talk sense into me. "Turns out, that's why he stopped running with me." Another laugh. "He was afraid I'd injure my delicate, pregnant self!"

I have to smile. Serena's never seemed delicate. Gorgeous? Yes. Lively? You bet. But fragile or dainty? Not so much. And now, laughing into my eyes, daring me to worry about her? Well, she's never looked stronger. Or more beautiful. So I relax into being happy about this best of all news.

"Do you think, I mean, can you tell if it's a girl?" I remember how it felt to hold Denver, to have an almost-sister.

Serena grins. "You, too, huh? Maze says he'll be happy either way, but I've been picturing her like you were when you were tiny."

"Come on!" I grab her hand and pull her over to where Mazen and my father are going on and on about their college days. "Let's tell Daddy!"

But my father and Maze have stopped talking about the past and started talking about the future. "Driverless is only a blink away," Mazen says, a finger in the middle of Daddy's chest. "I'm telling you, some of the mega-firms? They're already testing robot rigs on restricted routes—they're just not making a lot of noise about it, you know?"

Daddy turns, sees me. Maybe that's why there's a lot more up than down in what he tells his friend? "Not so fast," he says. He starts ticking off points on his own fingers, the way he always does. "First of all," he says, holding up his pointer, "who's going to unload these trucks?" He tells Maze all about the clumsy robots at the Western Wear warehouse. About the way you couldn't see the floor under that ocean of floating boots and boxes.

Daddy holds up his middle finger next. "Are bots like that going to auto-park and dock and do maintenance without human intervention?"

Why didn't my father mention all this to Red at the stop in Denver? I guess the comedy show those cowboy robots put on has made him feel almost as good about the future as I do.

Mazen tries to get a word in, but Daddy's on his fourth finger, and there's no stopping him. "What about flammable cargo, Maze?

Who wants to trade a seasoned driver carrying, say, gasoline, for a driverless bomb?"

"Speaking of bombs?" Serena drags me by the hand 'til we're standing in between them. "We've got some big news!"

"Oh, I know all about the low overhead," Daddy tells Mazen, as if she hadn't said a word, as if we weren't right there in their faces. "And the nasty habit truckers have of needing to sleep. But the thing is—"

"The thing is," Serena says, "I'm pregnant."

"See, service hours don't—" Daddy finally stops, stares at Serena. "You're *what*?"

Serena just smiles.

Daddy looks at me now, all questions. I nod.

Daddy turns to Mazen next, as if he needs to make sure we all agree. Mazen nods, too.

I'm pretty sure I've never seen my father so surprised *or* so happy. He's wearing a big clown grin now, silly and excited and loose as can be. He picks up Serena and whirls her just the way she was whirling me a few minutes ago. "I'll be damned!" he says as he spins her around. "I'll be hot and cold and freeze-dried damned!"

When he puts her down, he kisses her, then he kisses Mazen, and finally he picks me up, too. "We're going to be an uncle!" he tells me, whirling me so tight and so hard, my feet lift off the ground just like a little kid's.

Our celebration starts on the porch, where Serena shows Daddy the painting. Then we move inside, where we help get the biscuits out of the oven and wake up Serena's non-wonder dog, Shepherd. He's probably one hundred in dog years, and naps are his best trick. But we're making so much noise and we're happy-dancing so close to the kitchen table, which is his dog-cave, that he moans, barks, and finally struggles to his feet to see what all the fuss is about.

GOOD NIGHT, SLEEP TIGHT

"**H**ey!" Serena strokes her old dog. "Isn't there another pet that should be invited to our party?"

Okay. So I knew I couldn't hide Carrie in the truck forever. Even though I left her with extra water and Fuzzy Kitty treats, it's clear that Operation Keep Carrie has to include some tactics a little sneakier than just making sure she and Serena never lay eyes on each other. Besides, Daddy is giving me a parental nod, a sort of reminder that we have a deal: Carrie gets to choose.

I smile, as if I'm glad Serena reminded me, then walk across the street to the truck. Sure enough, Carrie is standing with her nose and both front paws against the glass, waiting. I open the door slowly so she won't fall out, then scoop her up and run back inside.

Maybe it's because she doesn't have to hide in my sweatshirt? Or maybe she's a bully who only picks on animals smaller than she is? Whatever the reason, Carrie is as good as gold in the house, and she seems to love being in this noisy kitchen with two new humans and one very large dog. There are no ducks to chase and no big crowd of tourists, so Carrie stays perched in my arms; she lets Serena stroke her behind the ears, bats at Mazen's high five with her paw, and yes, sits statue-still while Shepherd shoves his great big nose in her face and sniffs and sniffs.

Just as I was afraid she would, Serena falls in love right away. "Look at that white spot on her nose," she says. "It looks just like she's been scarfing down Cherry Garcia!"

I can't help laughing because that's the same thing I think every time I see Carrie's beauty spot. Now Serena puts her head close to Carrie's, and my kitten seems to be falling in love right back. She tries to turn over—even though I'm still holding her—so Serena can reach her favorite scratching place on her tummy. And of course, when I put her down and our hostess slips her a piece of hot biscuit, her purr motor starts right up. Operation Keep Carrie isn't exactly going as planned.

But it isn't until after dinner that I realize Carrie has an even bigger crush on someone besides Serena. When we decide to leave the dishes for later and go outside to stargaze, Carrie won't come with us. I look under the table and find her in Shepherd's cave, sleeping right between his giant paws.

"Hey, Carrie," I try. "Don't you want to see Mama Bear for real?"

Shepherd, who is sound asleep, doesn't move a muscle. Carrie does me the honor of opening one eye, but then she closes it again and burrows deeper into Shepherd's shaggy chest.

She's still there when we're all ready for bed. I try to pick her up, but she won't budge. Every time her back feet threaten to leave the floor, she meows like I'm killing her. I decide to leave her with Shepherd, but I make sure to tell her where I'll be. Right in my old room, the one I spent four years sleeping in. It's now Serena's winter studio, which means I get to fall asleep surrounded by bright canvases filled with flowers and sunlight. "I'm trying to catch the way the light changes hour to hour," Serena tells me. "See how the angle of the flowers as they follow the sun changes, too?"

I study the paintings, but mostly what I see is the way all the colors make a bright, winding wall around the whole room. It's like going to bed in the middle of a garden! Still, it feels strange to sleep without Carrie, but Serena makes things fall right into place by playing our old "Best and Worst" game. She kneels beside my bed and tucks me in as if I were still a little kid. "Bet I can guess the best thing in your day," she says.

"I'll bet it's the same as yours," I tell her. And we say it together, "THE BABY!"

"What's your worst?" I ask, and she doesn't hesitate.

"Those burnt biscuits at the back of the pan." Serena is an amazing cook, so I decide she's not kidding about being upset by something that no one else would even notice.

"Mine is the way Carrie looked at you and Shepherd," I confess. "I don't want to leave her here, you know?"

Serena smiles at me, leans back on one arm. "I know how you

feel," she says. "But I'm betting there's an old dying dog who doesn't want to let her go."

"*Dying?*" I sit up in bed. "Is Shepherd sick?"

"No, not sick." Serena stands up, hands on her belly now. "He's just old, that's all." She pauses. "Very old. The vet says he doesn't think he'll live past the summer."

I think of Scheherazade, her velvet ears, her red bandanna. I tell Serena how sad Heifitz is without his old friend. And then I think of all the grown-ups who have died—Daddy's mother and father, my mom, and maybe Willa's.

"I guess that's why the baby's here now." Serena isn't smiling, but she doesn't sound sad, either. "My mom used to tell me that every time you lose someone you love, an angel pushes a new baby out of heaven and into the world."

Now that I've remembered Willa, I tell Serena all about our hitchhiker. And that makes me remember Hollywood and my plans to put Daddy in the movies. I pinky swear her to secrecy and pretty soon I'm talking a mile a minute. I tell her about the scenes I've stashed away in my new "creative writing" notebook. Serena is lying in bed beside me, listening. Listening with a capital *L*. It's not just that she's quiet or nods or says "Uh-huh" once in a while. Instead, she gets all excited about what I'm saying and asks so many questions I know she's heard every single word and filed them away in her head or heart or wherever curiosity comes from.

"So, what's the ending?" she asks me now.

"The ending?"

"Sure, what's the last scene in *Wheels of Fire?*"

Suddenly I'm three years old again and Serena has just finished my bedtime picture book. All the toys and the little boy who stars in the story are going to sleep, and she's closed the cover.

"Does it really have to end?" I ask her now. "I mean, why can't we just keep trucking?"

Serena shakes her head. "Well, sure, but doesn't the audience need to know you'll be safe? That everything will turn out all right?"

"That's what sequels are for," I say. Serena smiles, says she needs to sleep for two, and asks could we wait for the sequels 'til tomorrow.

But then I remember something else, something important. "Serena, now that you're pregnant, do you miss your monthly?"

She laughs out loud. But when I mention what I've read in *New Body, New Self* she gets serious. "Are you telling me you've been wondering about all this on your own, with no other female to talk to?"

"Pretty much." When I emailed Yoly the Road Runner in Memphis, I got back an automated reply that was so not funny, I knew right away it wasn't really from her. "*On the road, so I can't respond now,*" it said. "*I look forward to getting in touch on my return.*"

"Well, we're going to make up for lost time while you're here, Hazmatazz." Serena yawns and gets up again. "But right now I think

I'd better take your future niece to bed." She turns out the light on the nightstand, which is actually an old drawing bench, and whispers close to my ear, "Sleep tight and don't let those pesky bedbugs bite."

"Sleep loose and tell them to vamoose," I say. Then we nose-kiss, and she leaves the door open a crack just the way she used to when I was a little kid and afraid of the dark.

I might not have headlights and air-brake whispers and the coming and going of a boxcars and reefers and flatbeds to put me to sleep. But I can hear the peepers starting up in the woods outside the window and a lonely dove that's so confused it's answering a barred owl's cry. *Who cooks tonight?* the owl asks, and the dove wonders, too: *Whoooo? Whooooo?*

They discuss this for longer than I can stay awake, and the next thing I know, it's morning and I'm getting a face wash from my favorite road cat.

A GOOD HAIR DAY!

"Does this mean you've decided to stay with me and Daddy?" I ask Carrie. But she's too busy washing my ears to answer. When she's finished, I run to the bathroom across the hall, and then we both head for the kitchen.

When we get there, there's no good smell of bacon or grits. Instead, Serena has set up two barstools by the counter, and she's wearing one of Mazen's tool belts strapped around her waist. Instead of screwdrivers and hammers in the belt's pockets, there are scissors, razors, and combs. "Can you shave one side of my head?" I ask when I recognize the styling tools. I'm so excited, I forget about being hungry and run out to the truck to get the magazine with the picture of the haircut I want.

But once I'm back, I realize the chances of my leaving here with hair like Cissy Mendez have just dropped to none. My father is already sitting on one of the barstools, a kitchen towel covering his neck and chest. "Hi, Daddy," I tell him with a lot less enthusiasm than most daughters probably greet their fathers on vacation.

Serena looks at the photo I show her and nods. But I can tell by the way she smiles at Daddy that they're going to dash my hopes. So I'm totally surprised when, brandishing a pair of skinny scissors and a comb around Daddy's ears, Serena asks me, "What color would you like?"

Okay, so they're not permanent, but the chunky hair chalk sticks she's put on the counter in a wine glass make me feel a whole lot better. When she's trimmed Daddy, Serena pins the towel around my neck and uses the chalk I choose to make awesome blue streaks that frame both sides of my face.

"Your hair is easy," she says, snipping a part right where I like it. "It just falls into place." She stands back to look, then points at her own head. "'Course, that means you miss the adventure of Black hair, hair that stands up for itself, that wants to go where it wants to go." She smiles, remembering. "My mother used to spend hours with me sitting on the floor between her legs, and her combing, combing, combing."

When my new look is finished, Serena hands me a mirror, and I can't help smiling, which kind of breaks the spell of the punk thing I've got going.

I glance up to see Daddy watching me. "I'm only eleven years old," I fake-scold him. "How can you allow me to leave this house looking so cool?"

Maybe it's because she's pregnant. Or maybe it's to celebrate our all being here together. Whatever the reason, after I sweep our hair clippings from the floor and Serena puts away her styling tools, she makes way too much breakfast for four people. There are buckwheat pancakes, cheese grits (it's a Southern thing), and sunny-side eggs on toast. Daddy scarfs down the most, and Serena comes in second. I slip one of my pancakes under the table for Shepherd, but Carrie the Walking Garbage Can snaps most of it out of my hand before that old dog even makes his way from lying to standing.

Mazen hates to have both his trucks empty and parked, but he always takes vacation time when Daddy and I visit. Still, you'd hardly know those two are off the clock. They're still talking trucks when it's time to stack the plates in the dishwasher. Mazen is telling Daddy about the ten-truck convoys he used to drive home with, and his voice picks up the deep purring sound that means he's talking about the good old days.

"I never did it often," he says, "but it sure was a special feeling, flying down the road with two trailers in front of you and seven more behind." He grins at me, because he knows that old song, "Convoy," is still number one on my hit parade. "Nothing like being hugged by your bros while you dodge gators and bears."

"Gators" are what truckers call pieces of tire in the road, and "bears" is their name for the police. I look at my father, and he knows what I'm asking with my eyes. "No," he says. "We can't do convoys. They're against the law."

I remember the scenes in all those trucker movies: rig after rig streaming down the highway in a row to fight for truth, justice, and fair play. "But why?"

"Because most people aren't as crazy as my friend here." He puts one arm around Mazen and uses the other to hold a glass up to the light. "And because," he says, adding the glass to the load in the machine, "I'm not the boss."

Part of it is that our CB's gone missing, and Daddy's never replaced it. The other part is, he likes to keep his own speed. "When it comes right down to it," he's always telling me, "I'm more slow-but-steady than flash-and-dash."

"Hey, in a few years, there'll be a ton of convoys on the road," Maze insists, trying to fit a gigantic frying pan into a too-small rack at the back of the washer. "Only they call it 'platooning' now. Trust me, it's the wave of the future. It's the coolest setup ever."

He forgets all about helping Daddy load the dishes and just stands there, looking at his private vision of the future. "The lead truck has a driver in it, and it's attached wirelessly to the row of robot trucks behind it. Europe's already running things this way, and, like I said, there are plenty of trial routes already crisscrossing this country."

A driver! They still need a driver! So by the time I get my license, things will be different. Gaddy and I will not only join convoys—er, platoons—we'll *lead* them. I won't need a CB, and I probably won't be telling the robot trucks behind me things like, "Copy, good buddy. 10-4." But Gaddy and I will be what drivers call "the front door," and we'll keep the pace nice and steady so all the trucks unload and pick up on time. Then I'll know what it feels like to be Burt Reynolds in *Smokey and the Bandit*, peeling down the highway smooth as a zipper, free to be happy, happy to be free.

It's easier to talk about Gaddy with Mazen than with my dad. Mazen likes convoys, and he loves to talk trucks. Pretty soon the dishes are done, and we're sitting in front of a pile of magazines, checking out the newest models. "Now that's some bang for your buck," he tells me, pointing to a cab with its own kitchen and breakfast nook.

"Here's one that memorizes four thousand hills in cruise control." I fold over the article, put it next to his fancy kitchen picture.

"When you're ready," he tells me, "we'll put together something that will knock their eyes out and make you Queen of the Road." Mazen loves rebuilding old semis, then tricking them out with every fancy extra he can find. (Which is how come Leonardo has a chrome sunscreen splashed across his front window and a sparkling wheelspinner on the steering wheel.) Maze's own truck is purple, with a trailer to match. And yes, chrome is everywhere—on the plate covers, the mega-loud train horn, the mile-high bumper, and of course the silver hunting dog on the hood. When he used to drive with Shepherd, he told everyone his dog had modeled for the statue. Now, of course, unless he can find a sleeping hound hood ornament, no one would believe it.

Lazy, crazy truck talk is the best. But we have only a few more days to spend together, so the four of us pack a lot of other stuff in, too—an Easter picnic at Duke Gardens; a concert on the front porch of The Carolina Inn; a trip to Jordan Lake, where we rent four stand-up paddleboards and each fall in only twice. (I make sure to ask Serena to redo my blue streaks once we're high and dry.) Mostly, though, we work in the garden and play way too much Monopoly. Our games all end the same way, with a three-to-one vote in favor of a rule "for the greater good of the community": Mazen is not allowed to own, or even think about owning, any railroad or utility.

And oh, yes, Serena and I finally have that "girl talk" about monthlies and sex and becoming an adult. It turns out growing up's not optional. "It's pretty much required," Serena tells me one night when it's just us getting ready for bed. "Like getting taller." She sighs, remembers: "When I was six? I decided to stay the height I was, so I'd always be able to share Meena's doghouse."

"Meena?"

"She was my family's Boston terrier. My father was allergic to dogs, so she was an outdoor pet." Another sigh. "My mom wasn't crazy about the extra laundry, but Meena and I had tea parties in her little house all the time. So I decided I'd never grow too big to crawl in the door. Of course, that didn't work out quite the way I hoped." She holds out one of her long brown arms and laughs. "But on the bright side, being bigger than dog-sized has meant I can do a lot of things better than I could at six."

"Like drive a semi?" I ask.

"Or paint bigger canvases." Serena knows about Gaddy, but she's never really been a truck person. "Your mom and I used to call our periods our 'power time.'" She stops, studies me. "Maybe that fancy book of yours didn't tell you how sisters get synchronized?"

"Get what?"

"It's true. When girls and women spend a lot of time together? They usually all get their periods at the same time." She sees me staring. "Way cool, huh? That's how it worked with your mom and me, we were always in sync. And when it was that time of month? We both ended up wearing a half shoe size bigger and tackling projects your dad and Maze told us were impossible."

I picture Mom, her red hair flying, and Serena, her Afro halo grown out more than she likes to wear it now (but which looks really good on her, even though she won't listen if you try to tell her that). I imagine the two of them clomping around in giant shoes, doing a sort of hard-core Riverdance.

"We got more done in those few days than in the whole rest of the month put together." Serena shakes her head, like thinking about it makes her sad and happy at the same time. "We even ran for town council once."

"You *did*?"

"Uh-huh. We didn't win, but we had a great campaign slogan." She points a finger at me and recites, "Sampson and Shields—Better Safe than Sorry."

I think about that Lady in the Moon face I saw the night I asked Mom about monthlies. And I guess I'm not so worried about growing up anymore. Because older doesn't have to mean a house and a pink bedspread. It could mean driving in convoys with Gaddy and taking breaks to come home to spend time with Serena and play with the baby. And yes, with Carrie the Traitor.

Every night now before bed, Carrie and I go through the same ritual. I carry her into my room and put her at the bottom of the spread. I slip under the covers and wrap my legs around her, just the way she likes it. I tell her not to let the bedbugs bite, and then I close my eyes. As soon as I do, I feel her weight shift and hear her jump down from the bed. In the glow of the night-light, I watch her rub herself around the edge of the door and then pour like dark syrup into the hall and out to the kitchen.

I don't even bother following her anymore, because I already know where she's headed. Right where I'm sure to find her the next morning: curled up beside her dog friend—whose ears she has thoroughly washed, and whose raspy snores must be a new kind of cat lullaby, since she sleeps with her own tiny ears as close to his slobbery mouth as she can get them.

For four nights in a row, Carrie has opted for sleepovers with that ratty old dog under the kitchen table. For four nights she might as well have been telling me loud and clear, "I love you, but you don't need me as much as Shepherd does."

ON THE ROAD AGAIN

On the morning of the fifth day, before anybody can quite believe it, it's time to get back on the road. This time, though, goodbyes are extra tough, since Daddy and I will be leaving without our road cat. It takes only one last look at Carrie, still asleep between Shepherd's long matted paws, for me to know I can't take her away from her new best friend.

Thank goodness we have an old best friend to look forward to seeing: Daddy and I want to stop in Lansing to check up on Heifitz, so Mazen has fixed us up with two bills of lading, the first for a pickup at a cosmetics warehouse in Detroit with a drop-off outside of L.A. (I figure my father told Maze I'm dying to become a movie star, and since Hollywood's the perfect market for eye shadow and lip gloss, it all works out!)

Daddy's got it all planned. We'll be studying the history of cinema on our trip west. And once we hit the City of Dreams, he's determined we'll spend a day as extras in whatever film we can find that needs two more faces in a crowd scene.

But if Leonardo will be hauling light on the way out, our faithful rig is going to be working harder on our trip back east. Daddy laughs when Mazen shows him what we'll be carrying from L.A. to Atlanta. He shares the second bill with me, and I read it out loud: "Item: six equine treadmills, Breeders' Gyms, Inc."

"Equine treadmills?" I read it again, wondering if we can be moving what I think we're moving. "Does that mean . . . ?"

"Yep." I think Maze takes on some clients just to tickle Daddy's funny bone. "I guess horses need to work out like people do." He grins at my father and points to the logo at the bottom of the bill. It's a drawing of a handsome pony with a flowing mane, galloping along a short rubber track. "On treadmills!"

It's a good thing we're laughing about horses and treadmills, since otherwise I might be crying about two-timing kittens and leaving my best female friend on the planet. The good news is that we'll be seeing both Carrie and Serena soon enough. But even though we're bound to be back for the incredible fireworks show Maze lights up the whole neighborhood with every July, the four of us stand on the deck hugging 'til we're all rumpled and teary. Then I watch them out the window as we drive off.

They hold each other's waists and sing "Happy Trails to You!" as loud as they can. They do this really dumb cancan dance while they sing, which makes it harder to leave because it makes me love them more. They get smaller and smaller in the rearview, and when I can't see or hear them at all anymore, I finally focus on my job: finding the quickest route I can to Lansing and Gyros.

We make it to the truck stop in record time and pull into the last space in the lot. We need to get an early start for Detroit tomorrow, but for now we're focused on only two things—seeing Heifitz and bingeing on dolmades. We're getting ready to lock up when someone pounds on my side of the cab. Then pounds again.

One of the first things you learn on the road is *not* to hammer on a driver's door. Sleep is precious, especially when folks are paid to get where they're going fast. Risk waking someone from a sound sleep and you risk an ugly scene—and maybe a fist in your face.

I see it's a woman who's making our cab shudder, and I guess she figures a kid won't punch her. Or maybe she's just desperate, but she keeps slamming on the door 'til Daddy nods and I open it.

"Hi, I'm Chilly, and listen, I know it's like dinnertime. I mean, no one else is around, and I'm sorry to get your draggy butts down here, but I need some frigging help, okay?"

Before I can answer, she's turned around and headed back to the truck parked next to us. It's a reefer with a giant banner spray-painted across its side. Pink letters spell out Sweet Scoops, the Ice Cream That Melts Your Heart. Chilly, who has a long blonde waterfall of hair tumbling down her back, is a blur now. She's racing back and forth from the freezer door of the reefer to dozens of big ice chests she's spread out across the parking lot behind her tractor. As she works, she's using language I don't hear very often, on account of Daddy and I only watch PG-rated movies.

When she notices Daddy and me staring, Chilly looks up. She isn't embarrassed at all by the swear words she's been using. She cocks one eyebrow at us as if to say, *What's your problem?* Then she asks us who we're staring at. "Hey," she tells us, "standing there is not exactly the help I had in mind." She wipes sweat (or melting pop juice, it's hard to tell) from her forehead. "Can you get over here and start handing these out?"

It's after Easter, and the sun is getting warmer each day, baking into all that asphalt. Which explains why Chilly, who's clearly the reefer's driver, looks so panicked—that and the puddles of chocolate, strawberry, and vanilla ice cream oozing over the sides of those coolers. Something (maybe a generator failure like the one that left Daddy and me without AC during a heat wave last summer) has cost her a whole shipment of the ice cream that melts your heart. Bars and cones, pints and quarts, even boxed ice cream cakes with flat tops and chocolate ooze coming through the flaps—they're all barely holding their shapes, just seconds shy of a puddle. "We haven't got much time!" she yells at us. And then, as we hesitate, "*Well?*"

It takes Daddy longer than it does me. I'm crouched by one of the coolers before he's moved at all. I load up with as many treats as I can, then follow Chilly, who tells me her real name is Cherie, between the rows of trailers. When other drivers, who are walking back to their rigs after dinner, figure out what's happened, they start to meet us halfway. They look like little kids, arms out, ready to collect their free snow cones or Eskimo Pies or Nutty Buddies. Everyone is grinning and laughing and saying thanks.

"Hey, the company's insured," Cherie tells them. Now that she's got help, she seems a lot more relaxed. "No biggie."

It's nearly a half hour before we're on the last cooler load, and honestly? By now it's like a giant tailgate party, only with no ball game and without cars. It's all trucks, and dozens and dozens of drivers standing outside their cabs slurping and chatting and grinning for all they're worth. It's an amazing feeling, dodging in and around all those semis, being met by applause and toothy driver smiles—and oh yes, the silliest "tips" ever. Guys are dropping keychains and gumball favors into my hand, as if they need to pay me back. One fellow, whose handle is Mad Maverick, trades an origami bird it must have taken hours to fold for two orange Creamsicles. He closes his eyes with the first bite. "Takes me back," he says. "Seven years old and pickup games."

The Great Ice Cream Giveaway is finally coming to an end. I've just handed off my last Sweet Scoops "special"—an ice cream sandwich with pistachio ice cream and a by-now-very-runny chocolate coating—when I realize Daddy still has nearly half a cooler to give away. I'm on my way to help him when I spot a figure across the parking lot. It's a girl talking to a driver who's about to pull out. A girl whose tilt of the head looks very familiar, who puts her hands on her hips in a way I remember oh so well. A way that dares you to tell her no.

I take off fast, determined to make it to her before she's hoisted herself into the cab. "Willa!" I yell it as loud as I can, cupping both hands around my mouth, using what Daddy calls my Megaphone Voice, trying not to lose steam as I run after her. "Willa! Wait up!"

A FRIEND IN NEED

When she finally turns around, Willa smiles at me before she can hide it. It's the world's tiniest smile, and it lasts only a second. But that second means she hesitates just long enough for me to catch up to her. I'm so surprised to be standing next to her, to be confronted once more with this scraggly half grown-up, I don't know what to say. But I haven't got long because the driver she's begged a ride with has both hands on the wheel and is watching us. One of his eyebrows is raised, half question, half challenge.

"Hi" won't work. And neither will "What's up?"

I tell Willa the only thing I know that will make her stop. "We're going to Hollywood!" I say.

Sure enough, she lowers her backpack.

"We pick up in Detroit tomorrow." I keep one eye on the impatient driver behind her, then go for the hard sell. "We're going to study films on the way out."

Willa doesn't say a word, but she turns back to the waiting trailer. She raises one hand, her fingers barely waving. He doesn't wave back, just shakes his head, shifts into gear, and takes off.

I let go of a breath I didn't even know I was holding. "Daddy says we'll start with the silent classics and stars like Mary Pickford, Charlie Chaplin—"

"Did you come here to track me down?" Her tee is as wrinkled as ever. And the old belligerence is back in her face and her voice.

"Actually, we came here to check on a friend." I feel a familiar anger. "A *real* friend." As soon as I say this, of course, I wish I hadn't. She looks like a little kid now, a hurt little kid. She picks up her backpack and starts to walk away, but I reach out, catch her elbow.

"Hey, I mean it," I tell her. "We're going to California, and my father says you can come with us." (Daddy doesn't even know Willa's here, but I'm pretty sure he'd agree to take her along if he did.) I don't get to hear her answer, though, because a familiar voice booms behind us.

"So!" I hear him before I see him. "You don't come to Heifitz anymore?"

Willa and I both turn as the old man, wheeling two huge garbage cans, walks toward us across the parking lot. "You see the world, but you don't tell Heifitz about it?"

I grin. Then I take one of the cans from him and the three of us walk to the row of dumpsters in back of the service station.

"We just got in," I explain. "We were on our way over when we had to help deliver ice cream." I tell him about Chilly Cherie and the melting ice cream. And then I remember to introduce him to Willa.

The two shake hands, and Willa acts different and sort of sweet with Heifitz. She tries to help by taking the other can, but he strikes a strongman pose, curling both biceps under his stained chef's coat. "From pushing this garbage," he says. "And eating all leftovers, what my dog don't no more."

I tell Willa about Scheherazade, and Willa tells Heifitz about her singing wonder dog Sasha. Before you know it, Heifitz is playing host like always. "You come inside now," he says. "Have lemonade."

I study the parking lot and find the Sweet Scoops reefer and Leonardo tucked in the last two spots at the end. I don't see my father or Cherie anywhere, though, so I tell Heifitz I have to go check in. I urge Willa to stay with Heifitz (that way I can catch Daddy up and sweet-talk him into giving her the longest hitch we've ever given anyone). I promise I'll be only a minute and then I take off, hoping to get back before (A) the two of them tell each other sad dog stories 'til they cry or (B) Heifitz makes those little honey doughnuts I love, and Willa pigs out and eats every last one.

But when I find Daddy, he and Cherie are still cleaning up the mess from the meltdown. They're inside the empty reefer hosing down the sticky asphalt, then stacking all the coolers outside. I feel bad that I didn't stay to help, but when I explain that Willa's back, Daddy understands. So does Cherie. Sort of. She insists she can finish Operation Wipe Up by herself, but she looks so hot and tired that my father decides we *all* need a lemonade break. He invites Cherie to Gyros with us. "Then we'll come right back and help you finish up here," he promises. "Deal?"

She isn't hard to persuade, and she decides to bring the last ice cream cake to the party. By the time she gets it packed in a cooler, I've left Willa and Heifitz alone for more than fifteen minutes. I'm worried, because in Willa Land, that's enough time for a giant tantrum or a fast getaway.

As the three of us walk to the restaurant, Cherie checks in with her boss, and I build up to the promise I've already made Willa. "You know," I tell Daddy, "Willa has changed." I check his expression without turning my head. (I don't want him to think I care.)

"Yeah, sure," Cherie says into her phone. "I already did all that."

"She seems, well, more mature."

"Really?" Daddy smiles. "That was fast."

"It's like she might not be so hard to live with anymore."

"I figure it's a bad coil," Cherie says. "You know, like in Fargo?"

Now Daddy's smile is full blast father-proud. "I don't think that's because *Willa* has changed," he tells me. "I think my daughter's found some extra room."

"Where?" Cherie asks her cell. "When?"

"Extra room?"

"In that big old heart of yours." Daddy pulls me close.

"Okay. Will do." Cherie pockets her cell and grins at us, and I know now is the time to kick my Adopt-Willa-for-a-Week campaign into high gear.

"So, you wouldn't mind if we helped Willa's Hollywood dreams come true?" I know Cherie doesn't have any idea what I'm talking about. But I also know my father is more likely to hang in low gear if there's an innocent third party around.

"You mean take her with us?"

"Yeah," I say. Cherie looks up, curious. I smile back at her. I do *not* look at my father.

The wait is shorter than I'd counted on. And Daddy's voice is missing the sputter, the indignant tone I'm braced for. "Maybe," he says, and now I stare at him, too surprised to answer. Then, with hardly enough time for a breath in between, he adds, "Why not?"

We find Heifitz and Willa in a booth at the back of Gyros. They're snug as bugs, talking like they've been friends forever, and they don't seem to have missed us at all. Sure, Willa's excited to see my dad, but she's just as happy to see the ice cream cake. And sure, Heifitz gets up to refill the pitcher of lemonade and to shake Cherie's hand. But as soon as we're all seated again, he winks at Willa. "Remember what I say." He puts one finger against his lips. "Tonight, we try."

The old Willa and the new one are jumbled up in my head. The way she lied to us just a few weeks ago doesn't fit with the happy-granddaughter smile she's giving Heif right now. Did I tell Daddy the truth before I even knew it myself? Has she really changed?

But I don't have time to worry about that now. Because, just as I thought, Heifitz has made Greek doughnuts, but miracle of miracles, Willa has eaten only half the tray he's put out. Cherie tries one and sighs like she's tasted heaven. "Stop me before I lick my fingers!" she says, and then she does it, anyway.

Now that I've been polite and let company go first, I take two for myself, and pretty soon, between the ice cream cake and the doughnuts, I'm in a happy sugar daze. I stop wondering if Willa is up to her old tricks. And I forget to remind her that we need to leave first thing in the morning for the pickup in Detroit.

When we finally hoist ourselves out of the booth and head back to hose down the reefer, Heifitz invites us to come back for dinner. Daddy and I are in, but Cherie insists she has to leave town as soon as her freezer "stops smelling like three hundred cows barfed in it." We all head for the door, and I turn to make sure Willa's coming, too. But she's not.

"I can't go with you." She's walks with me partway and stops. She's already engaged in some intricate sign language with Heifitz. I think it boils down to "I'll be right back."

"Why on earth not?" I'm borderline mad now. I've persuaded Daddy to take her with us clear to the West Coast, and she doesn't want to walk as far as the truck? She can't take the time to pitch in and clean up that giant mess?

"It's a surprise." Willa puts her finger to her lips just the way

Heifitz did earlier. "You'll see." She presses my arm, and her touch is friendly and warm, not at all like the girl who doesn't trust anyone. "Girl Scout swear."

Was Willa a Girl Scout? I try to picture her in a uniform, standing in front of a supermarket like the girls who sell cookies every summer. Girls who giggle and gossip together, who go home afterward and tell their parents how many boxes they sold. I try to mentally put Willa in one of those uniforms, but I just can't.

As I follow Daddy, Willa calls after me. "Oh, and Hazel?"

I turn around, half dreading what Scout Willa has on her mind.

"I love your hair!" She points to the blue streak I've been careful to preserve with the extra chalk Serena let me take on the road.

She noticed! As I catch up to Daddy and Cherie, I feel twice as cool as I did just a few minutes ago. And when they ask where Willa is, I cover for her. "I didn't see anyone in the kitchen," I tell them. (Which is true, even if I didn't look for Heifitz's dishwasher, or his prep chef, or any of the grateful strays he adopts as kitchen help.) "Maybe she's helping with the dishes."

Back at the trucks, I understand what Cherie meant about all those cows throwing up. It must be the way things have "steeped" while we were gone, but her reefer sure smells worse than when we left. She hands out rags and Borax ("This stuff beats bleach for deodorizing and cleaning," she assures us), and then we get to work. We hose down the whole trailer, scrub the walls and floors, and after an hour of hard, sweaty work, the smell has disappeared. We stow the rags, stack the coolers inside, and it's time for goodbye.

"I sure wish I could come to dinner," Cherie says. "But the company's made a service appointment for me to get this freezer unit fixed first thing in the morning. I've got three more hours of driving to make it."

She writes down her email and cell phone numbers on a Sweet Scoops business card. The way she slips that card into Daddy's shirt pocket and pats it afterward? I think she's definitely hoping he'll get in touch.

On the walk to Gyros, I level with my father. I tell him I have no idea why Willa didn't come back with us. "Unless she scarfed so many doughnuts, she got sick," I guess.

"Willa keeps her own counsel," Daddy says. He looks at my face. "That means it's hard to figure her out. I'm just glad we'll be able to keep an eye on her for a while."

Now I study *his* face. And suddenly I know why it was so easy to talk him into hauling Willa, as well as eyeliner, to L.A. "You figure on the way you can talk her into going to the police, right?"

He doesn't say yes, but he doesn't say no, either. And maybe he's right. I remember the way Willa can go from snotty teen to crushed little kid in two seconds flat. I remember how happy she was with a Tinker Bell toothbrush. Maybe she *does* need someone to take care of her full-time. Even if it's foster parents. I'm thinking about that toothbrush and getting all soft and runny inside when another Willa entirely greets us just inside the restaurant door.

She's wearing a green uniform and a white apron, and she's holding two menus. "Good evening," she tells us in a polished, grown-up voice I've never heard before. "Welcome to Gyros. Right this way, please."

AT YOUR SERVICE

We're out of words. Daddy and I just stare at the new Willa. Her hair is pulled back in a bun, she's wearing clear lip gloss, and—wonder of wonders—she looks squeaky clean. Did Heifitz dunk her in a tub? Did he threaten not to feed her if she didn't take a shower?

Willa has turned around now, and she's walking briskly and professionally toward the dining rooms. Still speechless, we follow her out to an enclosed porch, where the windows have been thrown open and a breeze is making it feel like we're outside. "I thought you might like some fresh air," she tells us, smiling, placing one menu in front of each seat at a small table with a view of the picnic area. (Which, considering where we are, is probably the most scenic spot in the house.)

"My name is Willa," Willa tells us. "Is there anything I can help you with before your server takes your order?"

Maybe Heifitz has gone rogue and locked the real Willa in a closet somewhere, and this polite, poised girl is an imposter?

Before we can answer, she's gone. We're left at our perfect table, staring around us in an empty room. Maybe Willa fell after our lemonade party, hit her head, and Heifitz revived her but couldn't cure her amnesia?

It turns out, though, what Heifitz *actually* did was offer Willa a job. "Is my new hostess," Heifitz announces when the two of them, breathless and excited, finally join us. "What you think?"

I look at Willa, who's moving our silverware and placemats to a four-top so we can all sit together. *Is this the same girl who was dying to be a movie star just a few weeks ago?* Daddy is watching her, too, and he seems even more confused than I am. "You know . . . ," he says slowly, cautiously, the way you'd talk to an animal you don't want to startle, ". . . it's hard to earn money when you're still supposed to be in school. There are rules, and—"

"Not to worry." Heifitz pulls out a chair from the new table, snaps a napkin across the seat. "No money, no money." He pulls out another chair, snaps it, too, then invites us to sit. "Allowance, maybe. But no salary."

"See, I don't need much at all as long as I have a place to live." Willa waits for both of us to take chairs, then she does, too.

"She stay with Zita, my Number One Dishwasher." Heifitz has it all worked out. Willa is one more lost soul he'll provide for, just like all the kitchen help he's hired over the years.

"Zita's got kids who need babysitting," Willa explains, "and a spare room in the attic. She showed me a picture on her phone. It's got a dressing table," she adds, as if she's describing a palace.

"With a glass top and so many fancy perfume bottles, I stopped counting."

"And here, got food," Heifitz reminds her. "Lots good food." He points his napkin at her. "You need fill up." He shakes his head. He folds the napkin in his lap, pats his stomach. "Too *kokaliáris*. Too skinny."

Willa grins as if he's paid her the biggest compliment in the world. She looks at me, beaming. "I'm kokolarios," she says proudly.

"This one." Heifitz points with his napkin again. "Just like Scheherazade. Love everything."

My father shakes his head, tries to make sense of all this. "Heif," he tells the old man. "This is a person, not a dog. You can't just step in and—"

"Help?" Now Heifitz is confused. "Why can't help?"

His question kind of bounces around in the empty porch. Because no one has an answer, not even Daddy. After all, Heifitz has been taking in strays, mostly of the human variety, forever. Yes, they've been older and some have bitten the hand that fed them. One fellow in Heifitz's ever-changing parade of dishwashers took off with his cash box, and a waitress once drove away in his beat-up pickup. (Although it broke down before she'd left town, so I'm not sure that even counts.)

A timer goes off somewhere; it's a faraway, tinny sound, but it sends Heifitz scurrying toward the kitchen.

"It's only for a few months," Willa explains to us while he's gone. "When I turn sixteen, I can get paid for work. And best of all, I'll get my license."

"License?" I have to admit, driving would probably be safer than hitching. Most truckers are teddy-bear soft inside, but like Daddy says, truck stops are not anyplace for a kid alone.

"Yep." Willa looks determined, happy, and full of plans. "The first thing I'll do is take a road trip. I'm going to drive back home and get Sasha."

"Is that safe?" Daddy asks the same question I want to.

"That's why I'm driving." Okay, make that determined, happy, full of plans, *and* very proud of herself. "My dad won't be expecting me, and I can wait in the car 'til he leaves the apartment." She makes a face like she's tasting something awful. "He keeps Sash tied up out back."

Operation Save Sasha sounds as though it belongs in our movie. It's daring and gripping, and I think Daddy and I should follow her in Leonardo. Just in case.

"Nice to have dog here again." Heifitz doesn't seem at all surprised by his new hire's scheme. He's returned with a huge tray full of dishes that make me hungry all over again. Willa helps him pass out the plates but keeps right on talking.

"Sasha will love it here," she assures us, as if the two of them have already discussed all this. "She's a real people dog." I guess the menus were just for show, because she puts one of just about everything in the center of our table. "She'd rather learn a new trick than play with other dogs."

"Maybe train Sasha dance to Greek music?" Heifitz is ladling huge dollops of tzatziki on everything and thoroughly enjoying himself. "Then we have elegant hostess, plus entertainment for your dining pleasure."

Since Daddy and I don't know what to say or think, we eat. All four of us devour one of the best meals I've ever had at Gyros, which means one of the best meals I've ever had, period. When we're finished, the restaurant's new hostess loads up a bus tray and heads for the kitchen. And that's when my father grabs the chance to level with Heifitz. "Are you sure about this, Heif?" he asks. "I'm still thinking we should take steps to keep her safe."

"Steps mean call police?" Heifitz waits for Daddy, even though we all know the answer.

Daddy lowers his head, sorry to say it. "Yes," he tells the old man. "I guess so."

"Paperwork," Heifitz says. "Judge in court. Rules." He smiles sadly. "I know all this, from when I bring wife from Preveza." He holds up one hand, spreads three fingers wide. "Three years it take." He runs his fingers through those silver locks of his. "This girl? This Willa?" He glances toward the kitchen. "She old enough by then, can leave without ask anyone."

I know this discussion is "for adults only." But I'd sort of like to remind my dad that Willa didn't have time to wait for paperwork and rules before she left her father. Sometimes you just have to move at the speed-of-kid.

"What about inspectors?" Daddy asks. "State labor laws? Child welfare?"

Heifitz points to the kitchen. "What about my dishwasher with no papers? What about my waitress with no address?" He turns, looks through the plateglass window at the traffic outside. "These people need job. Hard to start over in new country."

Daddy is confused. "So how—I mean, you can't just get the people in charge to look the other way."

The old man grins. "Heifitz cannot do this, no. But good, hot coffee? Food that drop like magic on their plate? Twenty-five years," Hefitz tells us. "In twenty-five years, no one make complaint, no one say law break." He picks up his glass of soda, holds it up to make a toast. "It take only few months to change this girl's life."

Daddy shakes his head, holds up his own glass. "I give up," he says. He looks at me, and I clink glasses with both of them.

Heifitz may not speak the best English, but Daddy says he talks more good sense than half the PhDs he used to teach with. It feels like something important, something good, has been decided, so I stand up from the table. "Maybe Willa could use some help right now," I say. I gather the rest of the dishes, find another tray on the waitress stand,

and head into the kitchen, too. I think Daddy and Heifitz know Willa doesn't really need my help. I'm pretty sure they both know I'm going to say goodbye.

"Are you positive you don't want to go to Hollywood?"

She's loading dishes onto the metal counter by the double sink, and she takes her time turning to face me.

When she does, she's wearing a big, open smile I hardly recognize. "He needs me here," she says. "He says I'm really good for the place."

I think about those studio tours they give in Hollywood. "I saved all your magazines for you," I tell her.

"You can keep them."

"Daddy says we can land extra parts in a crowd scene."

Willa shakes her head in this grown-up way, as if I'm a kid talking about make-believe.

"Don't you want to see if we can get on set at Nora Pearson's new film?" I remember how she drooled over the actress's picture, how she didn't want to turn the page.

"No, thanks." Willa takes the tray from me, stacks the rest of the dishes near the elbow of a skinny dishwasher with sweat leaking through his white paper cap. Then she takes *my* elbow and steers me back out the kitchen door.

"You know how long Mr. H was married?" she asks me. She stops before we reach the porch, as if what she's asked me is a precious secret, just between us.

I shake my head. "Over fifty years?"

"Fifty-five!" Willa is silent for a moment, contemplating this huge chunk of time. "Can you *imagine*?" But then she doesn't wait for my answer, just chatters on. "Her name was Adela, and she didn't really like dogs."

I nod. Heifitz has told me and Daddy over and over how his wife scolded him about Scheherazade. How she didn't think dogs belonged in the food business.

"But she loved little girls," Willa says. "She always wanted a baby, only they never had one. And me?" She spreads her hands across her apron, as if she's ironing it. "I always wanted a grandpa!"

I picture the Chinese Theater in downtown Hollywood, with all those stars' footprints in the sidewalk outside. I think about the bus tour to the mansions in Beverly Hills. And the wax museum, where you can take selfies with the most famous people in the world. But then I look at Willa's face.

And you know what? I don't think any of the things we'd do in L.A. could make Willa half as happy or excited as she is right now.

LA-LA LAND

Today Daddy and I are heading west by ourselves. It was hard to leave Willa behind, and I knew my father's worry engine hadn't really stopped as we got underway; it was on idle for the whole hour-long ride into Detroit. But just as we pulled into the warehouse there, I got a text from our former-hitchhiker-turned-hostess. Her message started and ended with a smiley face and in between was just one word, "THANKS," with a very long string of exclamation points after it.

I showed it to my dad, and I could tell it made him feel better, because even though we spent nearly two more hours waiting around for the lumpers to show up and load the twenty pallets of makeup we picked up, he didn't go grumpy on me. Instead, he started hatching plans for our study unit in Hollywood. So now we're heading to Chicago, and we're back to our old routine: my father's driving, concocting lesson plans, and I'm navigating, plus secretly working on my film pitch.

We're listening to *Carmen* full blast, and those songs are giving me lots of great ideas. I still don't know the words, but the fast music and that bubbly voice make me think about people who follow the sun. About brave truckers (and their navigators) who never get lost because they're at home wherever they go.

"Haz?"

I look up from my notes, which already fill half the spiral we bought in Denver.

"I've sent for a book on the history of film. But I think we should do some on-site research of our own."

I close my notebook so Daddy doesn't get nosy.

"Charlie Chaplin made one of his first silent movies in Chicago." Once my father is interested in something, he doesn't stop until he knows everything there is to know! "The studio building is still there."

I check the cell. "We'll be in Chicago by lunch," I announce. I double-check the screen to make sure. "Three hours and twelve minutes, to be exact."

"Good. Let's find a place to eat near—ready?" He waits 'til I've got a new search screen on the phone. "1345 Argyle Street."

"That's way uptown," I tell him. "Maybe we'll actually be able to park." Truckers, unlike the rest of the human race, can't just pull up and park anywhere we want, so we can't just eat anywhere we want to, either. It sometimes takes hours to find a place to berth a giant like Leonardo. And if we can't, we have to drive out of town until we find a truck stop where we can leave the trailer, then disconnect the cab and "bobtail" back downtown. (That's trucker talk for a horrible ride. Without a trailer for balance, cabs wobble and swerve and make you feel like your head is going to hit the roof every time you hit a bump.)

"See what you can find," Daddy says. "Anywhere in Chicago's going to be a challenge."

Of course, telling me that is just enough to make me determined to prove how much we need my navigational smarts. I start phoning all the places I'd like to have lunch. There are lots of noodle places around the address where we're headed, and I love pho soup. So I call every Vietnamese restaurant I find, rant about how noodle crazy I am, and ask if they know where we can leave our beast. One finally tells me they're not too far from an open lot by a construction site, and that two trailers have been parked there for several days. I take down the address. Then I hold up the cell, wave it at Daddy, and put on my cool, it-was-nothing voice. "Done," I say.

As my reward to myself, I spend the rest of the morning working on my movie pitch. I'm having so much fun describing our adventure with Cherie during the Great Meltdown, I start giggling and scribbling at the same time. Which means Daddy starts trying to read what I'm writing, which means I make a sorry excuse about needing more room and move to the bottom bunk in back.

It's not until we're in Chicago and I have to get us to the restaurant I picked that I notice how gloomy the sky's gotten. By the time we park Leonardo in the already muddy lot and hike the four long blocks to Crazy Pho You, the rain has started. And by the time we're inside feasting on some pretty fine pho, it's coming down in buckets.

Still, it feels kind of cozy and dreamy, stirring chunks of hot chicken and rice noodles while the world outside turns into a giant shower that's pattering (okay, hammering) against the window by our table. Daddy likes his pho with soybean curd (ewww!), but sometimes I think he orders it just to watch my face when he offers me a bite.

Our server is probably a few years older than Willa. Her name is Ngoc, and she makes sure we don't call her "Engoc," which is what it looks like her name badge says. She helps us pronounce it the way they do in Vietnam. (Well, as close as Daddy and I can get, which is "Nopp.") She tells us her aunt owns the restaurant and that she's working here to pay part of her way through school. And guess what? She's a student at the college that's bought what's left of the studio Charlie Chaplin used to work in, the very same historic, homeschool-type landmark we came here to see. But she has some sad news for us: When the college bought it, they gutted the place. Now it's just a big empty room that's been turned into an auditorium.

"It's nice enough," Ngoc says when we tell her why we're here, "but I don't think they left anything from the original." She sees Dad's face: he's stopped devouring his pho and looks deeply disappointed. "Sorry," she tells him. "The building's kind of pretty, though." She adds it like she thinks that will make things better. It doesn't.

"I was hoping there would be information about the movies

Chaplin made there." My father's not really stirring his noodles, just letting his fork drift. "You know, an exhibit and some old equipment from the period."

"There's a plaque outside, by the front door." Ngoc's voice has lost its perkiness, because by now she's figured out a plaque won't make the grade. "But inside? It's just offices and classrooms. I can walk you over there if you want," she offers. "I've got a class right around the corner from there in forty minutes."

So that's what we do. After our pho and a sweet rice pudding, the two of us follow Ngoc out the door. But we don't get far. In fact, it's all we can do to push against the wind and rain that's trying to force us back inside. It's like a giant shower turned up as far as it can go, and we're like ants trying to keep from being tumbled away. We close the door again and Ngoc shakes the water out of her braid. "We've got a few umbrellas," she tells us. "And I'll see if I can find some raincoats."

Daddy nods. "Get what you can. Then we'll all head for the truck, and we can give you a ride to class."

Ngoc grabs my hand. We walk back toward the kitchen, stop by a closet on the way. She hands me two umbrellas and a raincoat. "I don't think there's one big enough for your dad," she explains. I know it's pretty silly, but the umbrellas make me happy. Who needs their new hair color washed off in the rain?

We meet Daddy on the way. "Is there a side door?" He takes one of the umbrellas and explains that we can use the bigger building next door as a kind of rain shelter so we'll be out of the wind 'til we cross the street.

Not that we stay dry. But at least we feel more like people, less like ants. Ngoc juggles one umbrella and her books, and my father puts his arm around me and holds the other umbrella over us both. By the time we struggle the four blocks to the lot and race to Leonardo, we're soaked to the skin, and I know when I dry off, my towel will be covered in blue. Right now, though? My new do is not nearly as important as getting high and dry. We haul ourselves up and in, and we're all laughing and stamping with relief. But before Ngoc can check her books or we can even towel off, I notice movement in the rearview mirror.

That's when I realize that what's moving and flashing in the mirror is *water*! I open my window and look behind us. The construction site behind the parking lot has flash flooded and is filling up with rain. Worse, there's a small school bus—really a school van painted yellow and black like a school bus—sitting right in the middle of the muddy hole, and the water is already halfway up its tires!

"Hey!" I jump back down from the cab, run to the edge of the hole, and yell to the people-shapes inside the van. "Hey," I tell them. "Don't worry, we'll get you out!" I'm not at all sure they can hear me over the wind and rain. And I'm even less sure how we're going to save that little school bus. But I run back to our truck, call Daddy and Ngoc. "Come quick!" I tell them. I don't wait, though. I rush back to the lip of that giant hole in the ground.

The cement barrier between the lot and the construction site must have given way first thing; it's just a crumbling wall in places, nothing at all in others. It's easy to see where the van slipped into the water—a great big gap where the muddy ground is marked by fat tire tracks that disappear right over the edge.

The water has reached the bottom of the little bus's door. Inside, there's a woman and lots of kids. Hardly anyone is sitting in their seats. They're pushing the windows down, sticking their hands through, and yelling at me through the wind and rain.

THE CLIMAX!

By the time Daddy and Ngoc have joined me beside the ditch, at least one of the kids has pushed down his window enough to climb out. He's got one leg over the top and is ducking his head to squeeze through when my father yells at him to stop.

"Get back inside!" Daddy is definitely using his Megaphone Voice. Only, it sounds angry, as if the boy has done something wrong. But wouldn't anyone do the same thing as the kid if we were in that van—try to get out. *Fast.*

The boy, who's wearing what looks like a bike helmet, lifts his head to stare at my dad, and I'm pretty sure he's going to cry. But he lets go of the window frame and disappears back inside the bus.

"Should we get the chains?" I ask. "Can we tow them out?"

Daddy squints into the rain. "The angle's way too steep," he says. "Besides, even two feet of water can float a van that size." The kids are all yelling and screaming. "Or turn it over," he adds. "We've got to get them out fast." He studies the water, then makes up his mind. "We'll have to wade out with a towrope and let them follow it in."

Ngoc looks at the miniature whitecaps stirred up by the wind. Her dark bangs are already plastered to her forehead, and her raincoat is torn at one shoulder seam. She points through the downpour to the back of the little bus. There's a wheelchair fastened there. "How can they get out if they can't walk?" she asks.

That's when we figure out what the black letters on the van's doors, half covered by mud and rain, mean: UPTOWN CENTER, SPECIAL CARE FOR SPECIAL KIDS. A woman, who must be the bus driver, works her way over to the passenger-side window and calls out to us. "I've got nine children in here," she hollers into the wind. "Three can't walk, one has an inhaler, and two need head supports."

There's a long pause while Daddy, Ngoc, and I look at one another, then back at the woman.

"Can you help us?" she screams.

"Call 911," Daddy tells me. He hands me the umbrella, then runs for the truck. I make the call, and in what seems like only a minute, my father's back with ropes and a whole handful of bungee cords. Without an umbrella or raincoat, he's wetter than wet, and his red tee looks like it's made of shiny plastic.

He hooks two of the towropes together, then passes more ropes and bungees to me and Ngoc. "You two stay topside," he tells us. "I'll see if I can fasten the rope inside the bus, then throw it up to you." He ties one end of the cord to a piling at the edge of the parking lot, and he's about to lower himself down the side of the ditch into the water when he does the same thing the little bus must have done. The chewed-up concrete he's holding on to gives way, and he falls toward the muddy water. Like a mountain climber who's lost his grip, he clutches for support and misses.

He's under the filthy water for only a second, then he's standing knee-deep and trying to climb back out. Should I pretend that heroes don't swear? This one does, but in between *s*-words and *f*-words, he also moves fast—clutching at a new hold each time the rain destroys an old one, shooting pieces of concrete from under his hands in a shower of pebbles and grit.

As if coming out of a trance, Ngoc and I run to the edge of the hole, where Daddy is now sitting in the black water. We grab his arms, pulling his wringing-wet shoulders above the top. Finally, panting, he manages to lift his whole body out of the ditch and crawl back to where he started. I look toward the kids, still out of their seats, still pressed to the windows. Some of them are cheering, like they're watching a movie or a TV show. I'm kind of glad they're focused on us and not the water that's creeping up the sides of their van.

"Sorry about that," Daddy says. "I think I just put myself out of commission." He's turned himself over and pushed up to a sitting position. But he's rubbing his left ankle in a way that makes it pretty clear he won't be able to climb back into the water. "Any sign of the posse?"

I look across the lot and down the street. Nothing. No police cars. No passersby. No help.

"Why don't Ngoc and I give each other a hand down," I say, "while you make sure the rope is tight at this end?" He glances back to where he's tied the rope, and before he can stop us, Ngoc and I run along the top of the ditch to a place where there's no concrete at all, only mud. That's when she touches my arm. "You might want to take that cell phone out of your pocket first," she says. She's smiling in a way that doesn't make me feel *too* dumb.

"Thanks," I tell her, then turn back to hand our phone to my father. Hopefully if someone needs to reach us he'll be able to hear my very loud, very cool remix ringtone over the constant angry wail the rain is making. (Normally, that ringtone drives Daddy nuts, but right now I'm happy I chose something loud and proud.)

"Hazel." My father holds the end of the towrope with one hand, but he doesn't take the cell with the other. Instead, he looks at me long and hard. "If I'm the navigator now, you're in the driver's seat, right?" He sounds half proud, half worried.

I swallow hard, then nod. Finally he takes the phone and hands me the rope. "Do *not* let go of this. Understood?" By the time I grab my bungee cords again and crawl down the muddy slope after Ngoc with the tow, she's already closing in on the little yellow bus. Her knees are covered in swirling brown water that's chilly enough to take your breath away. It's nearly May, but we're in Chicago. This water is *cold.* As in freezer-compartment, numb-your-ankles, and make-you-want-to-turn-around-and-crawl-right-back-out cold.

The rain is still coming down hard, so I move cautiously, slowly, keeping a tight grip on the rope my father's also holding, trying not to think about hypothermia or losing my toes. I can feel the rope grow taut, and when I look back, I see Daddy has untied the rope from the wooden piling and is limping toward what looks like an old piece of rebar from the concrete wall. It's deep in the ground, and as he double-knots the towrope around it, the line grows even tighter.

By the time I reach the van, Ngoc is trying to explain to the driver what we need to do. The front passenger window is open, but the woman doesn't understand. First she tries to open the van's door, fighting the pressure from the watery ditch . . . and losing. Next she tries to take the rope I'm waving and pull it through the window. "No, no!" Ngoc yells. She grabs the section of rope I hand her and yells louder, as if that will help, "No!"

"That window's too small for the kids to get out," I explain. "We need to use the big window in the back." We gesture, we point, we clutch the rope and hop up and down in the muddy water. And finally, finally, she gets it. She heads to the back of the van and we slosh our way through the water to meet her, pulling the rope and bracing ourselves against the side of the bus.

When we get there, it's the driver's turn to pantomime. She points to the wide window, makes a cutting motion across her own throat. Points to the window again.

It's Ngoc who figures out her mime message. Or maybe she just finally sees the small red emergency handle. She reaches up, pulls it down, and the window springs open. It's well above water level, which is good. But it's so high up, it looks nearly impossible to reach. That's bad.

All the kids who aren't strapped into their seats are running around. It's clear the driver needs help, and if one of us were inside, we could probably make sure no one falls out a window or hurts themselves before we get them out. I turn around to look for my father. He's worked his way back to the edge of the ditch and is watching our every move.

"Someone has to get in there and fasten the towrope." I say it first to Ngoc, then cup my hands and yell the same thing to my dad. It's not a hard job, but I can see the driver is too busy, too rattled to handle it alone.

"I'm older. I'll go." Ngoc is standing beside me, and we're both holding on to the rope tight, tight. The wind has kicked up and the muddy ground under the water is uneven. Neither of us wants to fall, and truthfully? Neither of us is dying to climb in that bus window: it's pretty high up, and one slip could mean another twisted ankle for our rescue team.

Ngoc is slender, almost as skinny as I am. But she's slightly taller. "I'm shorter," I tell her, figuring I'll fit more easily.

Ngoc spits a damp strand of hair out of her face. "I'm heavier," she says. She puts her hands together like a net, holds them above the water.

"You win," I say, grinning even though I'm cold and wet and pretty scared. I cup my own hands around my mouth and yell to my father one more time. "Ngoc's going to help me up."

Daddy looks at Ngoc and then at me. "Go ahead," he shouts. "And Hazel Denise Sampson?"

Hazel. Denise. Sampson. The triple whammy.

Daddy yells back into the wind, and what he says next makes me feel like a cartoon superhero getting a power jolt. "You've got this, okay?"

I make an "okay" sign with my slippery fingers, then Ngoc and I lug the end of the rope under the window and the two of us hand it up to the driver so she can pull it through. Ngoc ties a bungee around her waist and clips it to the rope. "Hold tight!" she tells the driver. Then she makes a basket with her hands. I step into it, my own hands on her shoulders, and when I'm level with the window, I hoist myself up. Finally I throw one leg over, then let go and drop down the other side.

TO THE RESCUE!

It's easier than I thought it would be. I land on a bench seat under the window, and frankly? It's a relief to find myself inside this toasty bus. All those little bodies in this close space have warmed it up, and the din of the rain on the roof is softer, less scary than the torrents falling outside.

I wave at Daddy and Ngoc, then weave my way through the boys and girls, who seem really glad to see me. Most of them are pretty young, and all of them are very worked up. But they're more excited than afraid, some of them scampering to random windows so they can watch the water crawl up the side of the van. They point and laugh and can't seem to stop moving. They hold out their hands to shake, tell me hello, then ask me to play. I explain we can all pretend with the big rope I've brought. "We're going to be mountain climbers," I say, "and climb right out of this bus. Okay?"

I take the towrope from the driver, thank her. She thanks me, too, and we stand there, quiet, awkward. "What's your name?" she asks, as if knowing it will help. Somehow, the serious way she's asked makes me feel like she wants Daddy's triple whammy, so I tell her my full name, not my trucker's handle. "Hazel," I say. "Hazel Denise Sampson. What's yours?"

"I'm Julia," she tells me, smiling just a little now. "But the kids all call me Miss Julia."

Guess what? Julia was right; names help a lot. Pretty soon she's introducing me to the kids, and even though I can see the bus floor is getting wet, it feels important to take this time. "This is Melissa," Julia says, and I shake hands with a dark-eyed, maybe-ten-year-old in a Disney princess shirt. "And this is Andrew." A younger boy nods, pumps my hand up and down, up and down. "Meet Shirelle. . . . And Josie . . . and . . ."

Miss Julia and I move down the length of the van from back to front. As we do, most of the kids scoot into their seats just so they can stand up and shake my hand again. In between handshakes, I steal peeks at the water outside the windows and string the tow through the backs of the seats on the left side of the van. Up near the front, two girls opt out of shaking hands. Instead, they stay in their seats, looking straight ahead. They hardly seem to notice as I pass by.

Both girls are blonde and slender, older than the others. In fact, if they weren't so quiet and solemn looking, I'd guess they were almost-teenagers like me. After I wrap the rope round and round (and round again) the thick steel column of the van's steering wheel and make a double knot Daddy would be proud of, I pass by the girls again.

This time I see that they're both wearing neck braces, and the backs and sides of their seats have bulky rubber pads that keep them from turning their heads, so they only move their eyes from side to side when I come by.

I consider leaning in so they can see me better, shaking their hands. But I don't want to frighten them, and I don't want to slow down our rescue operation. Instead, I hurry to the rear window; I see Daddy standing on his one good leg, right where the rope rises out of the ditch. He yells to us across the wind. "One kid at a time, okay?"

Ngoc stations herself by the rope under the open window. "Ready when you are," she tells me, her legs wide apart, her feet dug deep into the muddy bottom of the ditch.

But in the bus? We're *not* ready. Not even close. Now that our welcome party is over and the novelty of shaking hands has worn off, the kids are up again and running around like crazed puppies. Julia and I smile weakly at one another, shrug, and get to work. We tell them we're going to show them how to mountain climb. They cheer and laugh and make more loopy circles.

Julia explains to the two girls in the booster seats that they need to watch us carefully, once we're in the water. We tell them they're going to mountain climb, too. They can't turn their heads, but they smile little half smiles, their eyes riveted on me and Julia.

I swallow hard, then take the hand of a boy wearing a helmet, the one who tried to climb out his window just a few minutes ago.

I've forgotten his name, so I ask it again. Maybe he's forgotten it, too, because he looks confused. But then he yells, "Mountain!" He makes a big, wild wave with the hand I'm not holding, and he looks very, very happy. "Okay, Mountain," I tell him. "Let's show them how it's done."

I explain about following the rope, about never letting go. And then I help him run his hand along the tow from the front of the van all the way to the back window. Ngoc is waiting underneath, so when I help him climb out and lean out to lower him toward the water, he keeps his hands on the rope. And Ngoc keeps hers on him. She scoops him up and holds him close to the rope so he can reach it. He clutches it, grinning broadly until he feels the water. Like I said, it's *cold*.

For a second, he stops smiling. But I remember about power jolts. I lean out the window again and yell, "You've got this, Mountain!" He forgets all about being wet. "Mountain!" he yells back from Ngoc's arms. And he keeps yelling all the way across the ditch. As Ngoc hands him off to Daddy and he's lifted out of the water and set on dry land, his smile is bigger than ever. Me? I'm relieved: one down, eight to go.

It's pretty much the same with the others—the ones who can walk, that is. The back window of the bus is well above the waterline, which, like I said, is good. But Ngoc isn't nearly strong enough to carry any of the kids that high. The water in the ditch is over her knees now, so when I lower a kid into her arms, she can't help but dangle their feet in the water. Some of them scream when they feel the cold rain on their faces and the damp seeping through their shoes; others are thrilled and happy, as if they're on a slide in a water park. Julia and I work with them one at a time, nudging each child toward the back of the bus, then helping them out the window.

Ngoc carries them beside the rope and lets them pretend they're doing all the work, whether they're touching it or holding it or just brushing their little hands along its length. Really it's Ngoc who's working hard, straining to hold a wiggly kid in one arm and use the other to grab on to the rope so both of them don't fall. When she reaches the edge of the ditch, the kids are way too worked up to take directions, so my father lifts them out of her arms, then walks them over to Leonardo, where towels and our truck's warm cab are waiting. Julia and I can see them now, waving from the windows, two of them struggling to fake-steer the giant wheel.

The rain seems to be slowing down, but the water is still rising up the side of the bus. The two girls who are strapped in their seats have waited patiently, but now, as if they understand how close the water is to floating the bus—or worse, turning us over, they've gotten flushed and fidgety. The one sitting nearest the aisle has tears in her eyes.

I kneel down beside her. Her hair is curlier than the girl's beside her, and her face is larger, more frightened. "Hey," I say. "What's your name?"

She can't turn her head against the cushioned guard around her neck. But she looks at me with a huge, glassy stare. She doesn't say anything, but she begins to smile, slowly, like a timid sun rising.

I reach out now and hold her hand, then tell her, "It's your turn to mountain climb. Miss Julia and I will help, okay?"

She still doesn't say anything. Maybe she can't? But she continues to stare at me, her eyes like magnets that stay and stay.

Julia walks over to us and adjusts the girl's seat, tightens the leg brace I haven't even noticed she's wearing. "This is Lily," she says. "Lily, this is Hazel. She's come to save us." Lily's expression hardly changes, but her eyes leave Julia's and travel back to mine.

Julia nods toward Ngoc. "Your friend is doing an amazing job," she tells me now. "And who's that by the truck?"

I tell her about Daddy's twisted ankle, how he's the one who made the towrope and decided how the whole rescue should work. Julia nods. "I'm sorry," she says, watching my father only a few seconds before she turns back to me. "But your friend can't haul these heavy booster seats across that water by herself."

Julia looks nearly as frightened as she did when I first climbed into the bus. "Lily has trouble unbending her knees," she says. I have to admit she's making me frightened, too. "And Maggie?" She nods toward the other almost-teen. "She can't control her arms or legs."

She's right, of course. How are we going to get two kids who can't even turn their heads or stand up out of this bus? And if we do, how will any of us carry them in these heavy booster seats?

HIGH AND DRY

I don't let go of Lily's hand. The way she tightens her grip around mine makes me feel braver, so I'm not really sure who needs who. "I guess some mountain climbers just have to climb sitting down," I tell her.

"That water's moving up fast." Julia's staring solemnly out the window, her voice newscaster-numb. But when she turns to me, she sounds younger, more frightened. "Does it feel like the floor is tilting?"

I study the view out Lily's window too. I watch a tire, along with a dented sign that says *No Parking*, drifting toward us. Across the street from the parking lot, there's a dog straining against its leash, barking furiously. It's strange to think that somewhere not far away dogs are standing on solid ground and life is going on as usual. But here, something bumps into the bus, and I nearly lose my balance. Could Julia be right? Could we be floating?

I check the tow I've run the length of the bus. It feels extra tight, as if something powerful is stretching it from outside. Sure enough, when I turn toward the rear window, our angle to the construction ditch has changed; instead of facing away from the parking lot, we're moving toward the side of the hole, tugging against that rope, trying to follow the wind. I sure hope the clamps holding the two lines together are solid. And that the rebar anchor Daddy ad-libbed stays put.

One thing's certain. We need to move quickly. More water has seeped under the doors, and already the floor is awash. I look toward the front of the bus, study the empty seats. I'm glad we've gotten so many kids out already, but it's clear we've saved the hardest for last. Still, that smile of Lily's makes me feel older, important. Suddenly, though, I realize Lily's not smiling at me and Julia anymore. Instead, her eyes have drifted toward the dog on the other side of the lot. It's still barking, but now when I see what it's barking at, I grin just like Lily.

"They're here!" I yell, a very happy banshee.

Julia looks up, and I point to the ambulance and fire truck just pulling into the parking lot beside Leonardo.

"Oh, thank God!" Julia brushes the hair out of her eyes as if she needs to make certain what she's seeing is real. All four of us are grinning now: Maggie, in the window seat, has caught Lily's glee, and Julia and me? We're smiling because we're proud of the kids, proud of each other, and because we've only now realized we're going to have a great story to tell. Well, maybe that's just me: Trucking Team Helps Save Kids from Watery Doom.

Julia is a different kind of happy. Pretty soon everything inside her spills over into tears and she's crying. "Up there?" She waves one hand toward the parking lot where a parade of people in yellow rain gear is heading into the water. "When I turned to avoid a pothole and lost the wheel," she says between sobs, "I thought I'd killed us all. I thought—"

I know what she thought. I put my hand out to touch her shoulder, and suddenly her head is burrowing into my neck, as if I were the grown-up and she was a scared child. We're standing that way when a man in a white hard hat bangs on the back window. Like the crack Emergency Team we've become, Julia and I stop talking and get ready for more action. She works to make sure the girls can be strapped into the stretchers the rescue workers are already passing over their heads, and I push open that back window again so our helper can climb in.

"Ladies," the man says cheerfully as he lets himself down to the floor. He's tall—taller than Daddy, and he has to stoop once he stands up in the bus. "You've done a great job." (Julia and I smile at each other, wordlessly deciding to save the high fives for later.) "But now that you're taking on water, I think it's time to desert your sinking ship."

Sinking? I look at our rescuer's boots and realize we're standing in several inches of water. Water that's turned our footing from slippery to splashy. Water that is slowly filling up the van.

"If you'll help me get these young ones onto the stretchers," he tells us, "I'll set you up outside so you can walk beside them." How did he know the girls would need that?

Julia has untied Lily from her seat and is using the bungee cords to fasten her onto the first stretcher. She has to turn the girl on her side so her legs will stay curled up. Next, she and I remove the blankets that are strapped to the bottom of the stretcher and fold them into bolsters on each side of Lily's body so she won't get hurt if the stretcher tips. The entire time we're working, Lily keeps her eyes on me. I'm not sure if it's because that's where she's facing once she's tied in, or if she's gotten used to me and needs something familiar to look at.

It doesn't really matter. Either way, her eyes on me feel good, as if I can do what has to be done. And I do. Julia and I help move the stretcher back toward the open window so the rescue crew can carry it across the water. Before they do, I hold Lily's hand and promise her I'm going with her. She smiles as if she understands.

So that's how it works. The crew waiting outside in the water help me out of the window as soon as they've got Lily's stretcher in position. Two men in hard hats and rain gear carry her nearly a whole foot above the ditch while I walk along beside them, one hand on the rope, the other reaching up to hold Lily's hand. She's not half as excited as the other kids were; I'm not sure, even though she's turned on her side in the stretcher, that she even sees the water swirling below her, though she must feel the rain on her face. It's tapered off, but it's still coming down.

When I look back at the bus, I can see the other stretcher being lowered and hear Julia and the worker who helped us talking to Maggie as they follow us toward the lot. I wonder, if those towlines weren't stretched tight, would the yellow bus be floating on its side or even upside down by now?

By the time Julia and I have joined Ngoc and Daddy, there's a small crowd across the street from the lot, and Leonardo has more passengers than have ever filled the cab—they are tucked into the front seats, bottom bunk, top bunk, and everywhere in between! There are soggy towels dropped on every flat surface, and the seven active kids from the Center feel like twenty—they're into everything, pushing every button and turning every dial they can get their busy hands on, opening drawers, throwing pillows, and fighting for the chance to sit on my father's lap while he blows the huge air horn.

I guess that's why we hardly hear the timid knock on the driver's side door, but someone finally looks up to find a small man with a camera crew behind him. So yes, we all get interviewed by the local TV station, and yes, the short, breathless interviewer calls us "heroes." In our movie, I decide, this low-key man will be played by a taller, louder actor, and he'll call us "daredevils." Julia is the calmest of us all. I guess now that everyone's safe, she's very grateful. She tells the interviewer that Daddy and Ngoc and I saved them all, and of course she can't stop praising the emergency techs who showed up just when we needed them most.

When the TV crew has left and Julia has called the kids' parents, it's time to let the ambulance team and the firefighters give everyone a ride back to the Center. Of course, no one wants to leave Leonardo. That is, until the firefighters drive their flashy red engine right up behind us. It's a good thing Leonardo isn't human, otherwise it might be hard to watch how quickly everyone forgets about eighteen-wheelers and goes crazy for fire trucks. After we've made the transfer and Lily and Maggie are safely loaded into the ambulance, Julia gives Ngoc and me long, soggy hugs. We promise to stay in touch, and Julia blushes when I call her a daredevil, but I think she likes it.

MY KINGDOM FOR A SHOWER

'm pretty sure it won't be a scene in the movie, but after Operation Rainstorm Rescue, our stars want one thing, and one thing only—a shower. Ngoc says it first: "That water was slimy and filthy and cold!" She looks around the empty cab. "Do you guys have, you know, a bathroom?"

Daddy and I look at each other, and I can tell by the way he nods that it's my turn to explain to someone about life on the road. "Not really," I say. "But we have this." I open a cupboard under our tiny, drinks-only fridge. Inside, keeping company with a dust broom and two rolls of toilet tissue, is a shiny white porta potty. "It's just for emergencies," I tell Ngoc. I pull out the bucket-sized toilet to show her the button that flushes it. "When you're sick, or you wake up in the middle of the night, you don't always feel like walking through a truck stop parking lot to get to the restroom."

Ngoc doesn't hold her nose, but she wrinkles it up, which I guess means she'd rather walk to the restroom. Then I tell her about the great showers at most truck stops, and the more I talk about the fresh towels and the hot, hot water, the more I wish we were parked at a mega-stop right now instead of wedged in between two rusty trailers in a rainy, muddy parking lot.

"I've missed my class by a mile," Ngoc announces. "So allow me to treat you guys to a shower . . . homestyle!" She grins at both of us. "My aunt's got only one, so you'll have to wait in line, okay?"

Okay? It's like Christmas and birthdays all wrapped in one! Daddy and I scramble around the cab gathering clothes and grabbing two fresh umbrellas for us all to share. Although by the time Ngoc has phoned her aunt and we're finally headed back toward the restaurant, we hardly need them. In fact, when I open mine against the sky, I can see a pale, watery sun trying to push through the last straggling storm clouds.

One short walk in a light spring drizzle and we meet Ngoc's aunt at the door to her apartment behind the restaurant. The three of us must look more like game show winners than flood survivors. We're so excited about showers that we're wearing broad smiles and acting like someone's just given us lifetime passes to Disney World!

After we're cleaned up and dried off, Ngoc introduces her aunt to the "heroes" who were on TV just a few minutes ago. Mrs. Tien doesn't speak much English, but she nods and smiles a lot, as if she understands what we say. When she talks to her niece, though, the two of them speak in Vietnamese. Right now they're having a conversation that is all music (no words) to Daddy's and my ears.

We listen, fascinated, and then Ngoc explains what her aunt has just said.

"My aunt thinks you are like Wonder Woman, Hazel, the way you climbed into the bus with the rope."

I smile at Mrs. Tien, and she smiles back. "But what about you?" I ask. "What about my dad?"

Ngoc and her aunt talk some more, then Ngoc reports back. "She says your father and I were very good helpers. She says that sometimes even Wonder Woman needs assistants."

Daddy high-fives Ngoc and then wraps his other arm around me. "All I know is that I was proud watching you both out there today. From my seat on the sidelines? You sure looked like heroes to me."

Ngoc's aunt puts one finger up and then hurries into the kitchen. "She wants you to take food with you for the road," Ngoc explains, then whispers more quietly, "She's going to load you down with twice as much as you can eat. Just do what I do, right? Say you can't wait to dig in, then make two or three meals out of it."

When Mrs. Tien comes back with two bags that smell like steamy pork heaven, I really *can't* wait! She smiles again, then she and her niece are back to chatting away in Vietnamese.

"Now that I've missed class," Ngoc explains, "my aunt wants me to help with dinner prep." My new friend doesn't look very excited about this last-minute assignment but grins at Daddy. "I can still show you how to get to that old movie studio, if you want?"

My father looks eager 'til Ngoc holds up one hand. "No promises, right? It's just a big, empty classroom."

Daddy nods. "Sure," he says, even though his eyes light up at the thought of seeing something he's researched and read about.

It's funny, but being used to goodbyes doesn't always make them easier. It just makes you know how badly you're going to miss someone. Ngoc walks us to the door, hands us the directions she's written on a Crazy Pho You napkin. When I picture her in the middle of that storm, hair streaming, bracing her small hands so I can reach the bus, I get all shy and sad.

"Be sure to send me the biggest, dumbest Tinseltown postcard you can find, okay?" she asks me.

I nod. First Willa decides Hollywood isn't that big a deal, and now Ngoc's willing to settle for a postcard. I nearly ask her to come with us, but I'm guessing her aunt wouldn't approve. Instead, I write down her snail mail address on another napkin and stuff it in my pocket. More hugs, and a few minutes later, Daddy and I are back to the soggy parking lot.

Even though the sun has made a comeback, Leonardo's quiet, damp-smelling cab still feels kind of lonely, so I'm glad it's only a short ride to the empty Essanay Studios building. Because my father is limping pretty badly, we leave the trailer in the lot and bobtail to Argyle Street. Where, sadly, the ghost of Charlie Chaplin is definitely *not* waiting for us.

Because sorry, Daddy, but Ngoc was right—the building is clearly just a college now, and the only thing left to remind people that dozens of famous movies were once made here is the plaque on the wall of the not-very-big Charlie Chaplin Auditorium on the ground floor.

We sit in the first row, just the two of us, in front of a big pull-down screen. We fold our sweatshirts in our laps, Daddy stretches his sore leg into the aisle, and we wait for a show that's never going to start. "Looks like the only films they show here are biology or chem videos," Daddy guesses. Which sounds about right, because I can see a marble counter under the screen. It's got test tubes and a sink built in beside the teacher's microphone.

"I'm sorry." It's all I can think to say. But Daddy laughs.

"*Sorry?* 'Sorry' says the young lady who just made me prouder than I've almost ever been?"

"Really?" I turn away from the screen where nothing's happening to look at Daddy, who's looking at me.

"You know who should be up on that screen, Haz? You! What you did today was epic. They should make a movie about you!"

For a minute I wonder if Daddy has found my Hollywood script. But then I realize he's not talking about that; he's talking about a movie in his head—a movie starring *me*.

"*Hazel Saves the Day!*" I grin and sweep my hand toward the screen as if the title was up there in giant letters.

"I mean it," he says. "You took charge today, you made decisions, you . . . well, you grew up real fast."

I laugh. "I've been doing that all along, Daddy. You just haven't noticed."

But Daddy's not laughing. "When I was a kid," he says, "my father wanted me to be a teacher. But I remember lying in bed all those years, falling asleep to the sound of traffic on the interstate. Listening to those big trucks and wondering what it would be like to live on the road."

I'm quiet, thinking about the grandparents I never met. The ones who never got to see their son become a professor.

"When you and I started trucking, I worried all the time whether or not I was doing the right thing."

"But now you're going to sit back and let Hazel save the day?"

My father's smiling again. "Let's put it this way," he says. "I'm going to worry a whole lot less."

By the time we pull into a truck stop off I-55 outside of St. Louis, we're both hungry and a little bit lonely. It's hard to go from seven wiggly passengers to none. Even though I've spent a good hour picking up soggy towels and scrubbing muddy footprints off our carpet, I sort of miss Lily and the rest of the kids. I promised Julia I'd email her whenever we stop and I can pick up Wi-Fi. She's going to put up a big wall map so the class can follow us across the country.

Daddy and I devoured our "takeout" as soon as we hit the road, so it's been hours since we've eaten. Before we head into the restaurant, though, I get out the laptop and send quick notes to Ngoc and Julia. I tell them that we've made it to St. Louis and attach a photo of the famous Gateway Arch downtown so they can picture Daddy and me at the very top. (We might not get there this trip since we're trying to make up time. But we've taken the elevator to that view of the whole city lots of times, so it's not like false advertising, right?)

Once you start missing, it's hard to stop. I check Willa's JimJam account, but the same old videos are still up. I guess she's too busy laying down plates to lay down new tracks!

But guess what? I spot at least four other JimJammers with videos I can't stop watching. They're all female truckers! Some of them are checking under their rigs' hoods. Some are just talking about life on the road. One of them is trying to dance in the cab of her truck. I send her an email to tell her how I love her funny, oh-so-tiny steps!

Then, because I'm still missing Willa, I send her an email, too, just to check in. At dinner I think of someone else I wish was with us. I remember how I always used to bring a leftover box back to the truck for Carrie. But since our Fickle Kitty has thrown us over for Shepherd, there'll be no one waiting for us when we've finished our meal and are all locked in for the night. No cat. No kids. No hitchhiker. No fun.

And no arch. This is what I was afraid of—Daddy tells me over our burgers that we won't be going downtown this trip. He figures if we stop to sightsee, we might miss one or both our drop-off dates. Whenever we run tight like this, the trucker part of him and the teacher part of him square off. Sometimes the teacher wins and we get to stop and learn. Other times the trucker wins and we whizz right through a major city (like St. Louis) without so much as a nod to what's special and worth looking at. (Like the brand-new stingray exhibit at the Saint Louis Zoo. It wasn't there when I was ten and we studied invertebrates, but now it's one of the best collections around.)

"If we don't push on this one, we'll let Maze down." My father is wolfing his double cheeseburger, as if eating fast will get us on the road again—even though we've already put in a full day and all it means is we'll get to bed earlier.

"Mascara? Really?" If we were carrying mangoes or chicken wings, I could understand the big hurry. But why should makeup mean I won't be able to send Julia and the kids a selfie from on top of the arch? "It's not like it's going to go bad, is it?"

"It's not just the makeup, Haz," Daddy explains. "It's those treadmills for the ponies. Turns out they're going to an equine rehab center in Atlanta."

I remember the two bills of lading. And I remember the way Daddy and I joked about gym-loving horses. "Rehab?"

"Horses that might otherwise have to be put down are getting second chances when they use treadmills underwater."

I put down my burger. "Did Mazen tell you this just to make sure we're on time?"

My father laughs. "No, it's true. If an injured horse has to carry a rider on its back, it might not be strong enough to do it. But underwater without a rider, it can get the exercise it needs to heal."

"Just like people, right?" I've seen videos of sidelined football players doing water aerobics, injured basketball and hockey players working their legs underwater before they get back to the court or the field.

So now, I remember Black Beauty and Misty of Chincoteague and all the other horse heroes in the books Daddy and I read when I was going through my crazy-for-horses stage. (I actually galloped instead of walking and ate onion grass when no one was looking.) "When they're healed, will they be able to run again?"

"Not always." My father's plate is empty, and he's already combing through his wallet for the right credit card. (Some are the company's, and some are just for us.) "The ones who've been really hurt might have to be put out to pasture or work as therapy horses."

I picture horses in white coats with stethoscopes around their necks. "Therapy?"

"Sure. Those kids we just left? Imagine how they'd love to ride a horse, old or not."

I nod. "They sure liked being mountain climbers, didn't they?" I picture the boy who yelled, "Mountain!" calling out "Hi, Ho, Silver!" instead.

"I think that's because they had a good teacher showing them how." Daddy puts down the card he's found and reaches for my hand instead. "And I'm not talking about that EMT, even though he was great, too. So what do you say?" My father's plate is empty, but I've still got half my burger left. "It will have to wait 'til we're back east, but wouldn't a selfie with those horses beat one at the arch?"

Me with my arm around a brave Appaloosa, getting back his will to run! A black stallion in a leg brace giving me a nose-kiss! The kids would love photos like those. And as a former charter member of the Misty Fan Club? So would I!

"Okay," I say, finishing my burger in a hurry. "Let's do this!"

WESTWARD HO!

Rinse and repeat: Hard driving, burgers for two, and *Twenty Thousand Leagues Under the Seas*. (It was Daddy's turn to choose, and even though this one's filled with way too many teachy sea facts, Captain Nemo is a pretty cool villain and there are some good, grisly murders.) That's how we spend the next three days, straight down I-44 to Tulsa and Oklahoma City, then out 40 through Amarillo, Albuquerque, and Flagstaff.

All the cities and attractions we pass by are just names on highway markers, a blur. Rodeos, goat farms, pueblos with powwows and dancing, water taxis, more zoos and museums—they all disappear in our rearview mirrors as we keep up the pace. Normally, I might feel cheated, but the fact is, Daddy's itch to make up lost time means I can write up the climax of *Wheels of Fire* so I'll be able to send our movie pitch out to the ten directors I figure deserve first crack at this future blockbuster. All ten have made action films, and they all think movies should be about people that matter. "My heroes aren't big names," one of them told an interviewer for *Boom!* magazine. "They're little people who do big things."

So I write. And write. Head down, under wraps, of course. I'm still not telling my father what I'm doing, and I'm pretty sure he thinks I'm taking notes on the material he's downloaded about the history of film. He's found articles about the very first moving picture ever made (of a racehorse), about how Thomas Edison made the earliest movies in America, and how modern directors film actors against a blue screen, then just fill in any background they want after. I keep our laptop beside my journal, and every twenty miles or so, I come up with a question that will prove I'm deeply involved. Just now, a few minutes outside of Phoenix, I cover my "notes" with the tablet, turn to him with what I hope is an eager, learning-hungry face, and announce, "It says here you can make an actual working camera out of cardboard." I wait 'til we stop for a light so he can see just how eager I am. "Can we make one and take selfies to send to Julia?"

Daddy beams. It makes me feel just the tiniest bit guilty about keeping my movie scheme secret. But then I picture how happy he'll be when we make a return trip to Hollywood for the premiere of our film. And how once we're famous, everyone will love truckers and we'll get pestered for autographs wherever we go. How we'll never have to stop trucking, and I'll pass my CDL, and Gaddy and I will—

"Haz?"

I stop daydreaming, slip my movie notes into the map pocket on my door, and check the cell. "We pick up 15 South and head to L.A. in 350 miles."

"I'm really sorry we've had to do this first haul like bandits," Daddy tells me. "That's not much fun for either of us." The light changes, and he moves Leonardo through the gears I've had memorized since I was six. (Everything shifts in an H pattern, and if you "float" the gears and make sure the RPMs are just right, you don't even have to use the clutch except to start and stop.)

"I'm tickled you're into this film unit." When my father's proud of me, his voice gets lower, softer. "I love the idea of making a cardboard camera, so let's be sure to ask for boxes when we drop off at the warehouse in L.A."

"Great!" I click through the articles he's downloaded. "I have the plans right here." I hold up the laptop. There are diagrams for three different models of pinhole cameras to choose from. One is made from a shoebox, one from a soda can, and one from a paper towel roll. I snap shut the tablet case, slip it into the map pocket, and check to make sure it covers my movie notes. That's when I see it out the window—a giant billboard off the exit up ahead. **ARIZONA OPERA**, it reads, **DARING. DIVINE. AND DOWNRIGHT DAZZLING.**

In much smaller letters underneath, there's something that turns my head. I slide down my window to make sure I'm reading it right. **Last Hot Ticket of the Season: CARMEN by Georges Bizet!**

My father taught Shakespeare. He loves books and old films, and he quotes poetry a lot. But in all the time we've been on the road, neither of us has ever gone to the opera. In fact, before I found out that Mom loved the aria Daddy and I listened to outside that auto parts store in Naperville, I thought opera was for little old ladies who need binoculars to see the stage. I figured it was like, well, pinhole cameras—something with historical value, but with no curb appeal whatsoever. Boring. Boring. Boring.

"Daddy!" *Carmen* was my mother's favorite, and now I have a chance to see it live! I grab my cell and search for Arizona Opera. "Look!"

Mom's show is right here in Flagstaff! All we have to do is pull over and take an exit downtown.

"What's up?" My father doesn't see the billboard, of course. And we're on top of the exit before he turns to me, half distracted, half curious.

"There's an Arizona Opera company," I tell him. "Their last show of the season," I read from the website I've found on the cell, "is the classic tale of love and jealousy, featuring the most famous free spirit in all opera."

Now, though, I spot the rest of the announcement, and Daddy must see how sad it makes me. "What's wrong?" he asks.

"The show's in Phoenix, not Flagstaff." I look at him, realizing it doesn't matter that we've passed the exit. Phoenix is an hour and a half out of our way, and my father's new speed-demon, no-stopping-for-fun road rules aren't likely to make that kind of detour possible.

Sure enough: "I don't think we can afford the time," he tells me.

"It was Mom's favorite," I say, feeling my throat close, the tears start.

"It was." Daddy isn't looking at me, even though traffic behind the next exit has us traveling at a crawl. "But those horses and the kids that will ride them are important, too."

Why is he being like this? His face looks like one of the stone gloomy pusses on Mount Rushmore.

"I know you want to see this opera," he says.

"I want to see *Carmen*," I say. "I want to see her stamp and be wild and beautiful and shake off all the rules."

I turn away from his stone profile and focus on the green box on our dashboard instead. *I want to see my mother. I want to see the woman who ran her finger down my nose and told me never to grow up.*

"I understand," my father tells the bumper-to-bumper four-wheels in front of us.

"No, you don't." My voice gets louder to stop the tears. *Are horses more important than* Mom? "If you understood, we'd take the long way, and we'd go see Mom's show."

"It isn't *her* show, Haz. It's about a free spirit in Old Spain, not an American grad student who wrote brilliant essays, but couldn't speak a word of Spanish."

I'm crying now, and I can't stop. This weird rules-first guy can't be my dad. I open the glove compartment, take out the photo of my mother in her rose blouse. "You just want her for yourself, right? You won't share her, will you?"

"Hazel!" Daddy finally turns to face me, only it's too late. Mom and I are already in the back of the cab. I curl up with the photo on the bottom bunk and howl like a baby. My father spent years with Mom, I got a *week*. And a marble box. The mother I talk to is a has-been ghost in photographs. Even as I hear myself wail, I'm still careful to hold my mother's picture gently; I can't bear the thought of tearing it.

"Hazel!" Daddy's voice is worried and hurt at once, but there's no way for him to pull over in this traffic.

Frankly? I'm too angry to care.

LOVE IS A WILD BIRD

'm squeezed into a ball just like Carrie. When there's a break in two lanes, my father finally stops Leonardo on the shoulder. "Hazel!"

I don't answer. I picture Carmen tossing her head. *Love is a wayward child, it never follows the rules.*

"Listen to me."

It's quite useless to call it, if it wants to refuse.

My father sits on the bunk beside me and puts his hand on my shoulder, but I shrink tighter into my ball. *Love is a wild bird that no one can tame . . .*

"There's something you should know." He sighs, and I hear it right through my baby sobs. "Sure, we need to make our pickup, but that isn't why I don't want to go through Phoenix."

I hold Mom's picture closer and scrooch as far away from him as I can. *If it suits it not to come, you can call it in vain.*

But Daddy isn't trying to touch me anymore, so I peek through my teary lashes and find him sitting at the end of the bunk, hunched into his own ball. "I—I just don't think I can sit through that story," he says. "It-it doesn't end the way you think it does."

"What do you mean?" I almost sit up, but then I remember how mad I am. "So how *does* it end?"

My father sounds really, really tired. I guess making up time has been a lot harder for him than for me. "You remember Don José?"

"Carmen's boyfriend?" He's the man who chases after her, who leaves his girl, his job, everything—all because he wants to be with her forever.

"José can't let her go, and . . ." My father sounds as if he's fighting his own words, as if he doesn't want to let them out of his mouth. ". . . she dies, Hazel."

"What?" Now I do sit up. I put Mom's photo in my lap and touch my curled-up father ever so softly.

"Carmen is murdered. In the last scene of the opera, Don José kills her."

"But why?"

"José doesn't want her to leave him, to run away with a famous bullfighter."

I look at Daddy. He looks at me. "But Mom would never do that," I tell him. I stare at the photo in my lap. "Not ever."

"I know." Daddy has lost his edges. If he were a painting, all his colors would be fading, dripping right off the page. "I'm so sorry, Kiddo. I just don't think I can do it. I don't—I can't sit through that."

"But Mom's *blood* made her sick, right? That's why she couldn't stay to watch me grow up, right?" That's why she had only seven days to hold me. And that's why she had to wear hospital gloves the whole time.

"Yes." Daddy shakes his head. Slowly, as if it's way too heavy to move. "It's not the way the opera kills her, Haz. It's that she dies, you see?" He rests his head in his hands now. "After so much life, so much fun and feeling and love . . . she's . . . gone."

"Why didn't you tell me?"

"I didn't want you to know how the story ended . . . not yet." He smiles at the photo, smiles at me. "Silly, huh?" Some of his colors are coming back.

"Very," I say. I study the picture in my lap. "When I thought you were choosing treadmills over Mom, I didn't like you much at all."

"I know."

"I loved you, but I didn't like you."

Daddy nods. He knows.

We skip Phoenix and we miss my first opera. Daddy promises to take me to *La Fanciulla del West,* a cowboy opera. "It has a happy ending," he assures me as we get underway. "And a cowgirl is the star."

I think about how important a happy ending is to my father. And how it doesn't matter much to me. I find his eyes. "Can I tell you something?" I ask. "Something serious?"

"Serious enough to pull over?" We're closing in on the City of Stars, and I know we're in a hurry. But I also know I need to tell him this while I've still got the nerve.

I stuff my notebook in the door flap. "Yes," I tell him. He downshifts and parks Leonardo on the shoulder.

This is not easy. "You know how you're always talking about 'resolution,' about the way a story needs to tie up all the loose ends?"

He smiles, nods.

"And you know how you plan on me going to public school?" I swallow, like part of me doesn't want to say what's coming next. "On us living in a nice house and sitting at the same table for breakfast every day?"

"Now, hold on." His smile gets crooked, and one of his eyebrows rises higher than the other. "I like variety as much as—"

I breathe deep and say it all at once: "I don't want to tie up our loose ends."

"But I never—"

"I know you think that's what's best for both of us."

My father takes his hands off the steering wheel, turns to face me. "I promised your mother," he says. "I promised I'd take care of you." He gets that remembering look. "I need to keep that promise, Hazel." He looks at his hands now, as if without the steering wheel, he doesn't know what to do with them. "I *have* to."

"You sound just like Odysseus," I tell him. Now I'm remembering, too—how much I loved studying the Greek hero of the Odyssey when I was just ten, how I hated to have all his adventures end—the trips to faraway lands, the monsters and nymphs, the cyclops and witches. "He made a promise, too," I remind my father, "but he forgot to check in with the person who was the reason he made that promise in the first place."

"What do you mean?" Daddy looks at me as if I'm the teacher now, as if maybe I got something out of the kids' version of that long, ancient poem we read, something he missed.

"I mean Odysseus promised Queen Penelope he'd come home. But I guess because she was a girl, he never asked her the most important question of all," I tell him.

That eyebrow of Daddy's is still raised like he's forgotten it's up there.

"He forgot to ask if she wanted to go with him!"

Daddy seems surprised. Too surprised to talk. He just sits and studies me, like he's trying to figure out who I am.

"I don't want a home that can't come with us," I tell him. "Or a perfect backyard or a school full of peers."

"But—"

"I don't need to make friends in my peer group."

"It's just that I want—"

"I'm sure you and Mom talked about giving me the best." Instinctively I glance toward the green marble box, as if it can help me explain. "But maybe the best is right here, right now. Maybe the best is happening every time we climb into this cab and start the engine."

"And cause duck riots?" My father is smiling now, not big and broad, but cautious and curious, with tiny wrinkles around his eyes. "And haul waterlogged kids out of floating buses?"

"Absolutely," I say. "And rescue kittens from plane crashes."

We're holding hands when Daddy tells me he needs time to think this all over. "It may take a while to give up the grill," he says.

"The what?"

"That three-story barbecue in our perfect backyard," Daddy says, grinning. "It was going to have a rotisserie and two burners. The grilling area could handle twenty-four burgers, and there would be stainless steel flavor bars to vaporize drippings right back into the food."

"Wow!" I say. He sounds just like Mazen describing one of his rebuilds.

"Plus LED lights for evening cookouts."

"Double wow!"

After a hug and a modified high five with an eighth move added, we're back on the road. The new high five now includes flipping an imaginary barbecue switch, and we're both sure no one else has seen anything like it. Or would have any idea what on earth we were doing. Good!

HELLO, HOLLYWOOD!

I keep writing and Daddy keeps driving. By the time we finally pull into a mega truck stop in Ontario, just half an hour outside of Los Angeles, I've put the finishing touches on my movie pitch. *Wheels of Fire* is finally ready for Hollywood!

It turns out, you don't need to write a whole script to tempt a director. Story Fixers, the company I found in one of Willa's magazines, promises to help you sell your movie "for more money than you've dared to dream of." All you need is a sample action scene and a high-powered, irresistible pitch letter. I persuaded Serena that twenty-five dollars was a bargain for Story Fixer's "Guaranteed Pitch Template," which she ordered and emailed to me yesterday, so now I'm ready to take La-La Land by storm. I've written down every pounding moment of our adventure in Chicago, and Daddy and I will be household names before you can say "happy ever after"!

Daddy's been hatching something, too, and he can't stop talking about our unit on movies. Even though I'm a lot less enthusiastic about our stay in Tinseltown than I was when I thought we'd be here with Willa, I nod and smile while Daddy goes over all the exciting stuff he's planned. He holds up one thumb. "Of course, we'll go to the beach first, like we always do." He's happy enough for both of us, so I just listen while he does that counting-on-his-fingers thing:

His pointer finger joins his stand-up thumb: "I've got tickets for two studios," he crows. Middle finger: "Plus, don't forget that crowd scene we're starring in." Ring finger: "The Walk of Fame and, naturally (pinkie), a picnic by our favorite waterfall in Griffith Park." He closes all his fingers into an air-pumping fist. "And we'll *still* be on time to pick up those horse treadmills."

"That's great," I tell him. And it *is*. I can see Daddy's put a lot of thought into our Hollywood stay. But I have something much more exciting on my mind. Like getting my movie pitch out to all those lucky directors. "So," I say, trying to make it look like I just thought of it, "can I do some emailing before dinner?" Actually, I never got an answer to the fan email I sent that JimJam trucker, and I don't need to write any of my road buddies, old or new. We planned on phoning Serena tonight, but if my father thinks I can't wait, what's the harm? "I'm missing Carrie, and I need to find out if the baby's kicked yet."

"Kicked?" Daddy tilts his head to one side, trying to remember. "Isn't it a little early for that?"

"Serena says it can happen at two months; she says she's already feeling ghost kicks."

Daddy laughs, stops remembering. "As in sort of there but not really, right?"

"I guess," I say. "As soon as she feels something and then tries to feel it again, it stops."

My father grins, but he doesn't say anything.

"The sign says free Wi-Fi," I remind him, pointing out Leonardo's broad windshield to the orange letters by the stop's check-in and game room.

"Sure," he says. "Lock up after your tired dad leaves to take a very long, very hot shower. Okay?"

As soon as he's gone and I've locked myself in with my laptop, I set a maddening pace in my one-girl typing marathon. My father says my keyboard technique is unique, and he may be right. I mostly use my thumbs, but once I get going, my fingers are a blur and no one I know is faster.

I copy my notes about our Chicago adventure from my film notebook. (The one with *GREAT AMERICAN NOVEL* printed in big letters on the front, and with everything inside written in my super-secret, pretty-much-illegible script.)

I don't mind typing it all out, because it lets me relive each thrilling minute of that afternoon. When Julia's bus lands in the huge trench and nearly washes away? That is *definitely* movie material! With every word I type, I'm more and more convinced that, like all the adventures Daddy and I have shared, this scene is the stuff that great motion pictures are made of. And best of all, there's no way a driverless truck, robo monster or not, could have done what we did. Only flesh-and-blood road warriors could have moved as quickly, carried as gently, or hugged as hard.

By the time I'm finished, I've gone through it all over again—the downpour outside Crazy Pho You, the little yellow bus in the middle of the construction ditch, meeting Julia and the kids, and, finally, helping carry them across the water to safety.

I can't wait to send this heart-stopping sample scene out to important Hollywood types who are sure to know just what to do with it. Of course, I'll include the oh-so-professional pitch letter Serena paid for and that I've fleshed with the cast and plot of *Wheels of Fire*. Next, all I'll need to do is worry about which offer to accept. Story Fixer promises that if you follow their ideas and the way they organize their letter, you'll have directors begging you to send them your movie!

Actually, if you ask me, those moments where Daddy nearly falls into the ditch and Ngoc and I are shuttling kids across knee-deep water are so dramatic they just about sell themselves. Still, to be safe, I copy the letter into the body of an email, then attach the gripping sample scene. I choose six directors' names to start. If they're going to be scrambling and fighting over my idea, I guess I don't need to send it to all ten at once, right?

As soon as I hit SEND six times (I don't trust that blind copy thing—what if one director finds out I've given others this once-in-a-lifetime idea?) and hear the comforting WHOOSH sounds that mean my emails are on their way, I start daydreaming. About how all six directors will offer to make Daddy and me stars. How we'll be household names: HAZMAT and THE PROF in *Wheels of Fire 2, No Passing Zone.* HAZMAT and THE PROF in *Wheels of Fire 3, Runaway Truck.* HAZMAT and THE—

"Hazel-for-crying-out-loud!" Daddy is pounding on the driver-side door. I scoot out from under the writing table I've pulled down over the bottom bunk. When I open the door, my father looks fresh and clean . . . and pretty mad. "What on earth were you doing back there? I don't have my key!"

"How come?"

"It's in the pocket of my old sweatshirt, which, sad to say, I—"

"—*left in the truck.*" Daddy and I say it together, and I hope he'll laugh.

Instead he just nods his head and looks ashamed of himself. "I looked for the spare, but—"

Uh-oh. We always keep an extra key under Leonardo's hood in case one of us gets locked out. Of course, when you get locked out and have to use the spare, you also need to remember to put it back. Guess who got locked out last week and forgot that last part? "Sorry, Daddy."

Now it's my turn to be ashamed. I hurry to take the pile of clothes he hands me and the smelly shampoo he refuses to be without. I make a big deal out of putting everything away, which also gives me the chance to turn off my tablet and hide my movie notes.

"So, what was so fascinating online that you couldn't hear your soggy dad when he wanted in?"

What I say: "I really needed to check in with Julia and the kids. I promised to send them selfies every place we stop."

What I don't say: *I did it! I finished our movie's climax! It will have audiences jumping out of their seats!*

What I add, when Daddy doesn't answer: "I can't wait to send them photos from Hollywood! Can we take cameras on the sets?"

What I don't say: *I can't wait to hear from those directors! Wonder how long before the offers come pouring in?*

I can't stop checking for emails from Hollywood. I check as soon as we get back from dinner. (Nothing.) I check the next day at the warehouse outside L.A., where we wait and wait and wait for the crew there to unload two rows and twenty pallets of eyeliner, lip gloss, and blush. (Still nothing.) I sneak my tablet into my backpack and check again when we park Leonardo at a rental car agency. (Nope.) I even check on the drive out to Venice Beach in our rental, a snazzy, bright red convertible—with a green marble box in the glove compartment! (Again, not a word.)

Venice Beach is nothing like Santa Monica, where we usually go. Santa Monica is a real family vacation beach, full of surfers and loaded with boardwalk amusements and rides. But Venice Beach is weird and crusty and full of magic. Daddy says the hippies who hang out there remind him of the way he and Mom dressed and acted when they first met.

Which means, I guess, that my parents wore crazy clothes and did just about anything they wanted to. Because that's sure what people all over Venice Beach are doing. We park the car just off the Speedway, a street that runs the whole length of town, and then we walk a block to the boardwalk along the beach.

Instead of roller coasters and rides, we pass men on inline skates with flowers in their hair and tuxedo jackets that flap out behind them when they zoom down the boardwalk. We stop to watch jugglers and acrobats who play guitars while standing on top of one another; ageless ladies with white hair and belly-dancer beads around their tanned, bikinied waists; two teenage boys (kind of cute) dancing to recorded music and wearing felt rabbit ears and rainbow-striped swimming trunks; a lady in a silver tutu dropping rose petals from on top of her stilts; a bearded man with a big potbelly and a live snake wrapped around it.

"Want to touch her?" the snake man asks me, unwrapping his pet partway and holding it out to me.

Daddy steps up behind me. "I don't think—"

But I'm already stroking the brown and yellow scales, and yes! The snake is already closing its eyes.

"Her name is Cynthia," the man tells me—only he says it like "*Sssssssssynthia.*"

Cynthia feels glossy and smooth, but not slimy. I want to ask if I can wrap her around me, but then my father puts his hand on my shoulder. "Wait." He looks at the snake's owner, points toward the ocean. "What's that noise?"

The three of us listen, and we all hear it—a low rumbling like thunder building on the beach. The snake man grins. "You'll see," he tells Daddy. "Just follow the crowd."

So my father, who isn't touchy-feely about snakes at all, hands me three dollars and asks me to give it to Cynthia's owner. "Thanks for letting me pet her," I tell him, and then Daddy and I turn around in the direction of the sound. It gets louder and louder, and we aren't the only ones who hear it. We take off our shoes and follow a whole crowd of people off the boardwalk and onto the sand.

The rumbling grows as we get nearer to whatever is thumping and booming down by the sea. As we come closer, we see more people ahead, dancing and waving on the sand, and now the noise they're making sounds less like padded bowling balls tumbling down an alley and more like wild, pounding music.

"What's going on?" Daddy asks a man in a jester hat who's racing by us toward the crowd. "It's the drum circle, man," the Jester yells back to us. When he turns, we can see he's wearing face paint. He's divided his face with a jagged line. One half is painted white, the other black. "Hurry up! You can't miss this!"

We follow him across the sand, stumbling to keep up. By the time we reach the fifty or so people gathered beside the water, the clouds along the shoreline are lit from behind, like blushing cotton candy. Everyone is facing the sun, some in chairs with huge drum sets or bongos in front of them; others standing to play guitars and didgeridoos, cowbells, maracas—anything that can keep a rhythm and pick up a beat. One girl not much older than I am holds an old-fashioned cereal tin and a spoon. You wouldn't think she could make herself heard in all that confusion, but she sure can wham and bam!

The Jester who led us here seems to know most of the drummers. And once he takes a flute out of his pocket and puts it to his lips, it's as if they're all following his lead. He dances around them, the black-and-white sides of his face blending as he spins. What he plays sounds like a music box on steroids, a tinkling string of song that slips in and out of the bongo's rapid patter and the base drums' deep, throaty thrums.

PEACE, LOVE, AND FOOT-STOMPING

At first the noise is overwhelming. I cover my ears, try to pick out individual sounds, but except for the flute, everything runs together. Somehow, though, after a few minutes, I don't care. I can see how it works now: the flute player started a beat, but then one of the really good drummers (the ones who are sitting down on the job, whose hands move like lightning over the skins of their drums) starts another, and then everyone else picks it up. Soon, another drummer changes it, and the whole group turns around like a flock of geese and starts keeping the new time. It's wild and fun and . . . *contagious*.

I start by tapping one foot; it's almost impossible to stand still with those drums booming out what feels like your own heartbeat. Well, *almost* impossible, for *almost* everyone. Except my father! Daddy and I are right next to each other, but when I glance over at him, I can see he hasn't caught the bug. Instead, he's standing, his arms folded in "watching" position, communicating to one and all that he has no intention of dancing like the crazy fools in the middle of the drum circle. Some of the dancers have costumes, like the forty-something guy dressed as a panther with a tail he keeps tripping over, or the mother and daughter in matching penguin suits. Others have just come from their boardwalk jobs and are still wearing aprons or can-I-help-you suits; still others are tourists and surfers right off the beach, in trunks and bikinis and fancy rash guards.

What's happened to Daddy's hippie past? Has he forgotten how he and Mom were flower children? Pretty soon, though, I stop father-watching and end up spinning and waving my arms like everyone else. That's when a group of kids comes over and dances all around me, then dance-naps me right into the center of the circle! Now, homeschoolers like me are not the best dancers in the world. We don't go to many (well, in my case, any) parties, so we don't know the moves. But guess what? It doesn't matter! No one cares. Everyone is doing their own dorky thing, and after a while I stop policing my feet and keep my eyes at smile level. I've spent so much time in Leonardo's cab, which is plenty big, as far as trucks go, but hardly wider than two people can reach with their arms joined, that looking out over an ocean without an end turns me weightless as a marshmallow, a cloud, a feather. Is that why I'm wiggling and shaking and pouncing and bending like a lunatic? Is that why I raise my hands toward the sky, then bring them down again, as if I'm lowering the sun softly into the sea? As if I'm helping it set?

Little kids, babies in their mothers' arms, teenagers, eighty-somethings—they're all either drumming or singing or, in some cases, doing both at once. But not Daddy. He's watching me (he always makes sure not to lose me in a crowd), but he's hugging the fringes of the circle. When I run back and try to pull him into the Land of Dancing Maniacs, he won't come. But at least he's tapping his foot now, which I know from personal experience means it's only a matter of time . . .

Sure enough, it's not me, but a boy in a parrot mask with turquoise wings strapped to his back who finally pushes Daddy over the edge. He takes one of my father's arms, motions for me to take the other, and together we dance Daddy from the outside of the circle into its sandy, crazy, sweaty center. Once there, my father takes cautious steps, his arms pinned to his sides; he's dancing, but he's also saying "excuse me" to anyone he bumps into or who bumps into him.

Then the beat changes; it gets faster—not bouncy anymore, but stamping and furious. That's when Daddy gets tired of saying "excuse me" and raises his arms above his head. He loses himself in the beat, turning like a rude tornado, crashing into one person and then another. He's leaping and gyrating, and everyone is laughing and getting out of his way.

I don't know if it's the drums or the flute music that's weaving in and out of them like a skinny ghost . . . but that's when I see her next to Dad—a lovely redhead in a peasant blouse with roses. She's the only one in the crowd who won't give him room. Instead, she dances right beside Daddy, matching his every crazy jump, every pinwheel turn. It's almost as if they're the same person and doing one of the silliest, wildest dances ever.

I try to catch my father's eye, but I can't. I don't think he's even looking where he's going. He's having too much fun; they both are. So I smile and close my own eyes and keep right on whirling.

We stay until the sun is below the horizon and a little dune buggy pulls up beside the drums. Two policemen get out and ask all of us to "disperse." The flute player in the jester hat tells us the drum circle gets shut down at sunset every day. "Why?" I ask as the three of us turn back toward the boardwalk.

"Near as I can figure it," the Jester says, the pale side of his face reflecting the red light on top of the dune buggy behind us, "things used to get rowdy, and since the whole point is to put the sun to bed, the beach patrol decided sundown is closing time."

"I have to tell you," Daddy says, "I haven't felt so good in a long time!"

"At least, not since Serena told us she was having a baby," I remind him. "And we did a group happy dance!"

"That was terrific for sure, Haz." Daddy turns to the Jester, whose hat is so full of bells, he makes music just by walking beside us in the sand. "But this was different." He shrugs, looks at the flutist, lost for words. "I stopped being afraid, I guess. Stopped worrying about the future, about getting old. All I cared about was—"

"—putting the sun to bed?" the Jester asks.

"Or just having a party?" I suggest. I remember the sound of all our feet thumping the sand like an invisible instrument underneath the drums. "I mean, it felt like we were all there to celebrate."

"Celebrate what?" my father asks.

"Everything!" I pump my fist. "Our new baby!"

Now the Jester is interested. "So what baby is this?"

Before my father can work his slow, careful way into the story, I tell our flute-playing friend about Daddy and me being in trucking; about Denver, who isn't our baby anymore; about Serena and Maze, whose baby is only a painting and a few maybe-kicks right now, but how she's going to be real enough to hold by November!

"She?" Daddy is smiling.

"Yep," I tell him. "We're going to have a girl. Serena and I have decided."

We've reached the boardwalk, but instead of saying goodbye, my father walks us to a bench and offers to get ice cream for all three of us. "My thanks for showing us the drum circle," he tells the flute player. "What'll you have?"

Daddy takes orders (I want butter pecan and the Jester wants, yep, you guessed it, chocolate and vanilla), then he crosses the boardwalk to a store that sells ice cream and zillions of postcards. I watch him join a long line of people waiting to order.

I turn to the flute player. I tell him Daddy's and my trucker's handles. Drivers don't usually give each other their real names, so I don't ask for his. But he tells me anyway. "I'm Lancelot Gobbo," he says. "Pleased to meet you, Hazmat." He gets up from the bench, takes my hand, and bows low like someone in an old movie.

The setting sun is right in my eyes. I put on the sunglasses my father calls my "navigator specs." This time, though, I'm not squinting to see highway signs, I'm checking the ice cream store. Daddy hasn't even reached the front of the line. There are still three people ahead of him, and one is a woman who's leaning over the counter like she's arguing with the man behind it. We've got some time.

I remember how Lancelot's music opened doors with every crazy step we took, and how every time we danced through one of those doors, we found something wild and true on the other side. So I turn back to our new friend. "Will you play some more?"

Lancelot smiles, creasing his painted face. He takes the flute out of his pocket. Now that I'm close to it, I see how beautiful it is. It's made of wood, and there's a small, intricately carved wolf howling near the top, just where Lancelot puts his fingers on the holes. I'm studying the wolf, listening to the first notes he plays, and then?

I'm gone! I've sailed away somewhere in my head, lifted off and left the boardwalk and the beach and even our red convertible tucked into that crowded, dusty parking lot. I can't tell you how, but the song Lancelot plays holds me like a hug, picks me up, and I hear feathers, I see hearts beating, and I touch the white spot on Carrie's nose. When he stops playing, I can't bear it. "More!" I beg, like a little kid, a baby that's had her toy taken away. "Play it again!" Then I remember I'm not a baby. "Please?" I say.

Lancelot shakes his head, smiles again. "Sorry," he says. "I never play the same song twice."

"Why?" I can still hear those feathers. My fingers are still deep in Carrie's fur. "Why not?"

"That feeling's gone," Lancelot tells me. "And a new one's taken its place. Want to hear it?"

I nod. Lancelot puts the flute to his mouth and plays again. What I hear is nothing like the music he played a minute ago, but it picks me up all the same. This time I taste bubbles of laughter, and I hear the way Mom's red hair whispers and curls and wraps around my face. She takes my hand and we dance in a dry riverbed, cracked and empty, until the rain comes down. The sky opens up like a smile and the water pours down, and when the music stops, I realize I'm crying.

"Haz? Earth to Hazmat!"

I open my eyes and my father is standing by the bench with three ice cream cones in a cardboard tray. "Where's our Jester?" he asks.

Like someone coming out of a dream, I look at my dad. I'm kind of glad he can't see the tears behind my sunglasses. Then I turn to the empty space beside me on the bench. Lancelot Gobbo is gone.

FORSOOTH, WATERMELON!

"**L**ancelot Gobbo!" My father is pulling out of the beach parking lot when I tell him the flute player's name. I've been talking nonstop, even while we finished those three drippy cones (Daddy and I shared Lancelot's) and all the way back from the beach. But now he stops and stares at me. "That's the clown in *The Merchant of Venice*!"

"*The Merchant of Venice?*"

"It's a play of Shakespeare's," Daddy explains. "We haven't gotten to that one yet."

"Shakespeare's Lancelot what's-his-name is a court jester?" I ask. "He wears a hat with bells?"

"Not really," Daddy explains. "He's more of a natural fool. I'm pretty sure no one pays him to be funny."

I think about the way Lancelot disappeared before Daddy got back with our cones; about the song he played. "I wish you could hear it!" I tell my father. "I wish everyone in the world could hear it!" I'm beginning to wonder if I made the whole thing up, but I can still hear the music in my head.

"Hey," Daddy smiles because I'm smiling, like he can't help it. "Just looking at your face when you talk about it is a trip, Haz." He reaches across me to open the glove compartment, checks on the green box, closes it again. "Now, let's say hello to Hollywood, okay?"

We drive to a Super 8 near Universal Studios. When we can't stay in Leonardo, we choose small hotels like this one, where the rooms are big but the price is low. (Mazen always tells us to treat ourselves, but Daddy likes to keep expenses down.) Actually, I'm not sure if the room we walk into now is large or if it's just that, after living in a tractor's cab, anything feels roomy. We've got two queen-size beds, a mega-screen TV, a walk-in closet with an ironing board, a desk, and free Wi-Fi. In other words, we're in Trucker Heaven!

It feels strange to be putting Mom's green box in our room's closet safe. We both know she's too big, too beautiful, too much fun to really fit inside that marble box. And storing the box in a closet? It's sort of like putting a tumbling bouquet of roses in a jelly jar and then hiding it in the dark. But we've always protected her this way, and it's kind of hard to break the habit.

So Daddy slips the box into the safe and we both say the combination out loud together: 662231. Maybe it's ourselves we're taking care of, after all. But it makes us feel better.

And hungrier. We order room service, which takes forever to arrive but gives me time to check for emails from Hollywood. At first I see the same old nothing: junk mail about truck insurance or "deep discounts" on service or new trucking apps. But then I spot a message that's not an ad or a freebie. It's from willamette@sonicboom.com.

It's Willa! And yes, she's still rooming with Heifitz's dishwasher and working at being the best hostess she can be. Which must be pretty good, because Heifitz has already told her that all the customers love the service. Before she signs off, she catches me up on my JimJam videos, which, it turns out, she actually put online. I haven't been offered a movie contract, but at least someone likes my impersonations of hood ornaments:

> Yull never believe it Hazel do you remember the videos
> I took of yu on yer dad's truck???? I posted them and yu
> already got 25 likes! 😎 😎 😎 xxx W
> PS I am gelous!!!

I'm pretty sure it will take more than twenty-five likes to persuade a perfume company to make a cologne with my name on it. But I tell Daddy how great Willa's doing, and once dinner arrives, I'm too focused on fries and butterfly shrimp to worry about missing out on my own signature scent. By the time I'm finished, I'm also too full and sleepy for TV. I get first dibs on the bathroom while my father watches the news, and then we do our Baby Bear/Papa Bear routine. Only tonight, we just say the words from our beds because the only glow on our ceiling is coming from a blinking red light on the smoke alarm. My dad makes a joke about "red giants," and then, before I have time to come up with one about "blue dwarfs" (we did an astronomy unit last fall, but mostly I just remember the constellations and the stories Daddy told me about them), I'm drifting off. I dream of bears that twinkle and a special secret they ask me to keep. I tell them I'm the best secret keeper in the world, and I am, because the next morning, I have no idea what the secret was!

Daddy is already in the shower when I wake up. He always takes his shower first because he says I'll use up all the hot water if he doesn't. (I don't bother asking how he figures I could use a whole motel's worth of water. I think that's just something his mother used to say, and he likes to repeat it.)

I plug the tablet into an outlet between the beds and think about what a strange day we had yesterday. I remember how Lancelot vanished, and I wonder once again if maybe I made him up. But I couldn't have, because Daddy saw him, too. Besides, that last song of his, the one Mom and I danced to? It's still playing in my head. Only now it feels like Mom and I have stopped dancing and are lying on our backs, laughing and letting the rain fall on our tongues. Which is how I nearly miss the email. It's from henryblaz@rockcastle.com. At first I don't recognize the address and I skip right over it. But when I go back and read what it says, my breath catches:

Dear Hazel Sampson:

I am intrigued by your proposal. It is fresh, compelling, and could make for an uplifting film. I am confident that, in the right hands, this story could become a cinematic benchmark, a turn away from cartoon superheroes to everyday, living legends.

Yes, I'm referring to you and your father. The two of you will be valuable consultants to our production team, should we purchase rights to the material you sent. Which is why I'm inviting you both, on behalf of Rockcastle Studios, to visit us in Hollywood. We will provide expenses, comfortable housing, and, if focus groups respond in sufficient numbers, an option agreement which will allow you to enjoy an extended vacation from life on the road.

Naturally, you will need to wrap up any secondary commitments. Trucking, traveling, and public appearances unrelated to *Overdrive* (the new title our promotion staff has agreed on for your splendid little narrative) will not be possible while you are with us, or under the terms of any contract we might offer you during that time.

Said contract, of course, will give our script experts the right to fine-tune your characters and story in order to make a film America will take to its heart.

Congratulations, and welcome to Hollywood!

Henry F. Blazer, D.G.A.
For Rockcastle Entertainment, Inc.
Los Angeles, CA

You know how you can wish for something so hard that you forget to think about what you'll do when you get it? I stare at the screen, watch the cursor blink beside Henry Blazer's name at the end of the email. I can hardly believe it's actually happened—we've got a really, truly offer from a grown-up movie director whose last two movies were advertised in *Star News* and who did an interview with *Boom!* magazine! I look at the letter again and all I see, as if they were in bold type that pop off the screen, are the words "living legends" and "Welcome to Hollywood!"

I want to read those words to Daddy. I can't wait to tell him the news, watch his face as it soaks in—we're not just *touring* Hollywood. We're not just going to be extras in a crowd scene. We're going to make a whole movie. A movie all about *us*!

I rush to the bathroom door, but I can still hear the shower running behind it. Maybe that's a good thing, because when I come back to my tablet and read Henry Blazer's email over, I see other words, ones that weren't popping off the screen a second ago. I see "indefinitely," "comfortable accommodations," "wrap up secondary commitments."

My breathing has settled, and the shower's still churning away. I read the letter a third time, and that's when I realize what those other words mean: "comfortable accommodations" means a house with a barbecue and a bed with ruffles. "Indefinitely" means Daddy and I would have to give up trucking and move to Hollywood.

If we accepted this offer to visit Tinseltown, and if that visit led to a movie deal, it would end our life on the road faster and surer than any nightmare robo-truck ever could. I would never get to take the CDL or buy a rig named Gaddy. We would have to "wrap up" our "secondary commitments" by starting every new day in the same old place. We'd be superheroes, all right—phony, dressed-up has-beens who'd forget what trucking is really about.

I don't know how much longer Daddy's shower will take, but I know I definitely need to talk this over with 662231. I recite the numbers out loud as I press the keypad and the safe opens.

"Mom," I say. I remember Lancelot's music, I remember Mom and me tasting raindrops. "I have to ask you something." I touch the green marble, but I don't take the box out of the safe. "Quick, before Daddy comes back." My mother already knows about *Wheels of Fire*, of course. So I tell her about the once-in-a-lifetime, impossible offer we just got from Hollywood. I tell her about "indefinitely" and "*Overdrive*." I tell her how I hoped our movie would destroy robot trucks, make people love flesh-and-blood drivers. But now, I'm not sure. Now—

The bathroom door opens, and Daddy, smelling all perfume-y and wearing a fresh tee and jeans, is very surprised to see me sitting on the carpet in the closet by the safe. We stare at each other, both of us embarrassed. It's Daddy who makes it better. He smiles through his confusion. "Girl talk?" he asks.

I smile back. "Why do you smell like gardenias?"

"I left my shampoo in the truck back in Ontario." He holds out his hands and pulls me to my feet. "But I left you plenty of hot water, and if you hurry and get your own shower in, we can tread the boards."

"Boards?" I ask.

"*Treading the boards,*" Daddy explains, "means walking onstage. Did you forget we're due on a movie set this afternoon?" He moves in front of the window and, backlit there, strikes a pose, one hand held high, finger pointed, as if he's giving a speech. "Watermelon," he tells me. "Watermelon." Next, he turns to face the window, his other hand up. "Watermelon," he repeats, looking through the glass toward downtown L.A. "Watermelon. Watermelon. Watermelon."

I crack up. *What is he* doing?

"I'm acting," my father explains, as if he's read my mind. "This is what movie extras say when they're in a crowd scene and they have to pretend to talk."

I hold up my own hand now. "Watermelon," I say.

"Or sometimes rhubarb," Daddy adds. "It could be rhubarb, too."

How does he know *these things?* "Rhubarb," I try, and it feels much more elegant than watermelon. "Rhubarb!"

I exit email, zip up the laptop case, and still laughing, put it in the closet inside the safe. "Help me answer this, okay?" I whisper before I close the safe door and grab a clean tee and cutoffs. Meanwhile, Daddy has obviously decided that two is better than one. He's busy alternating both versions of crowd talk: "Rhubarb, watermelon," he chants. "Watermelon, rhubarb."

I head for the bathroom. "Okay," I say just before I shut the door. "Keep practicing. I'll be ready in no time."

"Ha!" My father snort-laughs. "The way *you* take showers?"

I hear him mumble something about using up every vegetable from cauliflower to zucchini, but it doesn't matter. I'm in my happy place now—no movie offers, no glowering robo-trucks, just hot water and bubbles and me, singing off-key.

NO THANK YOU

By the time we leave the motel, both of us freshly showered and smelling of gardenia shampoo, it's too late for lunch. We head to the studio lot for our "debut," as Daddy keeps calling it. The whole drive over, we rehearse our crowd talk, and we decide that my father will say "watermelon" to me for the whole scene, and I will continually reply "rhubarb." It turns out, though, we don't get a chance to say either one.

The studio is huge like a town, with streets and offices and lot after lot where homes and parks and restaurants have been recreated, and where scenes from several other movies and TV shows are being filmed today. A few days ago, Daddy got an email with a long set of instructions for "Extra Special Talent." It gave us directions to the studio, told us not to call attention to ourselves during shoots, and said we should wear "casual street clothes" for our "urban crowd scene." Our jeans are perfect. I notice we're dressed like everyone else, as about fifty of us take an escalator down to what looks like a real subway stop. We're supposed to be people who pass by a group of buskers on the way to our trains. The three buskers are played by real actors (not famous ones, but still . . .), who get paid; the rest of us are either underpaid (background actors) or doing it for free like Daddy and me. (My father registered us with an agency that supplies huge crowds of innocent bystanders, football fans, or frightened tsunami victims whenever scripts call for them.)

The assistant director, who's the one in charge of extras, chooses about ten of the paid background actors to look at the musicians curiously as they walk by. He selects another three to drop some money in their hat. But he tells the rest of us that we should just walk right past the players without even looking at them, as if we're used to passing them every day on the way to work or school and are in a hurry to get home.

Sadly, our veggie talk is no good to us at all: the assistant director tells us (three times, in a very stern teacher voice) that when the director calls "ACTION," the musicians will play, but everyone else on the set has to be stone quiet (yes, he actually says "stone quiet") so that the mic will pick up only the music, not background noise.

Not a single rhubarb or watermelon passes our lips, and all Daddy and I can do, if we want to pretend we're talking to each other, is to make believe we're silent movie stars and go into pantomime mode.

It isn't long, though, before I forget all about being a silent film star or even moving through the crowd. I can't stop staring and I can't stop listening. Because after the guitarist and the banjo player start a tune, the third busker takes a flute out of her shirt pocket.

She has red hair. She sounds just the way Lancelot did when he joined the drums, wrapping her music all around and through what the others are playing. Like a firefly or a fairy, darting in and out of their song, she weaves it together with a silvery shimmer that won't stay put. I can't help it, I close my eyes. Right there, in the middle of a phony subway tunnel, where I'm supposed to keep walking. I stand still, and you know what? I can hear my mother singing. She sings like I do—not well, but like she means it. And because she needs my help and I need hers, I sing with her. Loud and long.

It's as if there's just her music and the two of us. It's not like Lancelot's music, with doors opening everywhere. Instead, it's like Mom and I have shut out the rest of the world. The words we sing are like a dream, and as soon as I say them, I forget them. There's something about hating songs with a chorus, something about never singing the same song twice.

Pretty soon, the extras who were walking through the set a few seconds ago, the ones who had stopped to listen, even Daddy—they all disappear behind my closed eyes, behind the fun, the craziness of singing so loud and so hard, with someone I feel I've known forever. By the time the poor flutist is shocked enough to stop playing and the other buskers put down their instruments, too, I open my eyes. And the assistant director yells. He's almost as loud as Mom and me. And a lot more angry.

You guessed it: Daddy and I are asked to leave. It's not Daddy's fault, of course, but where I go, he goes. So we're back in our little red convertible before we even get our free meal in the actors' cafeteria. And we're back to the motel's parking lot before he finally asks. "What was that all about, Haz?"

It was all about that email on the tablet I left upstairs, in the closet safe. It was all about knowing what I want to write back. I take a deep breath, let the car and the twilight outside it disappear. I need to know my father is behind me 100 percent. "Daddy," I tell him, "there's something I have to ask you."

He doesn't say a word. He just waits.

"If I could buy us a house of our own, right this minute." I stop, correct myself. "Well, maybe tomorrow. If I could make sure it has a barbecue and a porch like Serena's and a two-car garage."

Daddy nods, still waiting.

I take another breath. Then I ask what counts: "Would you trade it for what we have now?"

My father doesn't answer right away. He takes his time, like he's really thinking about what I've said. Then he chuckles, takes the key out of the ignition. "Can you promise me more songs like the one I just heard from you at the studio?"

I'm very close to touching my ears with the sides of my smile.

"And will you do your share of the driving when you get your CDL?"

"My share?" I laugh out loud. "Does leading platoons count double?"

My father gets out of the car, waits 'til I come around to his side before he locks it. "Let's cross that automated bridge when we come to it, okay?" He holds up his right hand for our new crazy high five.

"Deal," I say. High. Low. East. West. Elbow. Elbow. Clap. Flip that barbecue switch.

Back in the room, we decide to have dinner downstairs, but I announce that I need to do some email catch-up before we go. I take the laptop out of the closet, whisper thanks to Mom, and set up at the desk. While my father, who is tired of smelling like gardenias, uses the GPS to find the nearest drugstore, this is what I write to the studio:

> Dear Mr. Blazer:
>
> I am honored by your offer. I am sure your studio makes heartwarming films. But I am sorry to tell you that my father and I have decided that the best way to remain living legends is to keep on trucking.
>
> We will not be accepting your offer of comfortable housing or living expenses.
>
> We will not need to wrap up our current secondary commitments. And you will not need to worry about finding out what focus groups think of us, or about buying our story.

I hope you don't feel bad about this. Good luck finding your next blockbuster,

Hazel Denise Sampson

Chief Navigator

Shields Trucking

After I push SEND, I wait for the WHOOSH and then I close my eyes. Inside, where no one can see it, I feel a party starting up. It's not the loud, foot-stomping kind on Venice Beach, or the happy dance we all did in Mazen's kitchen. It's quieter than that, a kind of deep *thank you.*

Which might sound funny, since I've just said *no thank you* to fame and fortune. I've passed up our big break, what Daddy would call our "date with destiny." But you know what? I'm not one little bit sorry. Because saying no to destiny means saying yes to whatever comes next: to watching ponies tread water. To a dog-rescue road trip with Willa. To teaching Serena's baby girl the words to "Convoy." To Daddy and me and Mom frying the circuits of every robo-truck we meet. And most of all, to never playing the same song twice—to a story full of crazy, nest-in-your-heart characters and a new setting every day, a story that keeps right on growing and changing with no resolution in sight, without ever tying up loose ends or coming to

THE END.

NO BOOK

That's what I'd have without the help, skill, and beautiful souls of:

♥ my delicious and brilliant editor, Jonah Heller, who's been a compassionate collaborator and inspiring interrogator from start to finish;

♥ my writers' group and dear friends, Marjorie Hudson, Karen Pullen, Donna Washington, and Frances Wood, who hold nothing back, and are all in, all gold;

♥ my "Dear Mailbox" and Beta Reader Extraordinaire, Uma Krishnaswami, whose writer's heart is the safest place I know;

♥ my splendid, savvy agent, Ginger Knowlton, at Curtis Brown, Ltd, who read my draft as soon as I sent it, and who thanked me for keeping her up reading on New Year's Eve!

♥ and last but far, far from least, my entire Peachtree "support team": Amy Brittain, meticulous copy editor; proofreader Rebecca Behrens; Oriol Vidal, whose cover helped me "see" what my heart felt; cover designer, Maria Fazio, and art director, Adela Pons; and two very special readers from our Penguin team, Nicole White and Todd Jones.

Deepest gratitude to all.

ABOUT THE AUTHOR

LOUISE HAWES is a teacher and the author of more than a dozen novels for readers of all ages. She has served as Writer in Residence at The University of New Mexico and The Women's University of Mississippi. She was also a John Grisham Visiting Writer at the University of Mississippi. Louise helped found the MFA program in Writing for Children & Young Adults at the Vermont College of Fine Arts and currently teaches there. She researched much of this book "on the road" in her home state of North Carolina and reports that, at 5'2", climbing in and out of 18-wheelers is a great workout! Follow her on Twitter @louisehawes; on Instagram @hawes252; and visit her on the web at *LouiseHawes.com*.